ON THE ORIENT RAPIDE

I had half-closed my eyes, contemplating the promised breakfast...when the door at the far end of the carriage swung open. In stepped a figure wearing a white and gold military tunic, handsomely tailored with Austro-Hungarian flair, and the sash of nobility across his bemedaled breast.

I respectfully rose to my feet. Count von Tarnhelm had extended his hand in what I took to be a gesture of democratic fellowship. As he drew closer, I realized the outstretched hand gripped a Colt revolver aimed at Vesper's head.

"Please retain your seat, Professor Garrett. I suggest all of you do likewise," said Dr. Helvitius.

BOOKS BY LLOYD ALEXANDER

The Prydain Chronicles
The Book of Three
The Black Cauldron
The Castle of Llyr
Taran Wanderer
The High King
The Foundling

The Westmark Trilogy
Westmark
The Kestrel
The Beggar Queen

The Vesper Holly Adventures
The Illyrian Adventure
The El Dorado Adventure
The Drackenberg Adventure
The Jedera Adventure
The Philadelphia Adventure
The Xanadu Adventure

OTHER BOOKS FOR YOUNG PEOPLE

THE XANADU ADVENTURE

LLOYD ALEXANDER

PUFFIN BOOKS

PUFFIN BOOKS

Published by the Penguin Group

Penguin Young Readers Group, 345 Hudson Street, New York, New York 10014, U.S.A.

Penguin Group (Canada), 90 Eglinton Avenue, Suite 700, Toronto, Ontario, Canada M4P 2Y3
(a division of Pearson Penguin Canada Inc.)

Penguin Books Ltd, 80 Strand, London WC2R 0RL, England

Penguin Ireland, 25 St Stephen's Green, Dublin 2, Ireland (a division of Penguin Books Ltd)

Penguin Group (Australia), 250 Camberwell Road, Camberwell, Victoria 3124, Australia
(a division of Pearson Australia Group Pty Ltd)

Penguin Books India Pvt Ltd, 11 Community Centre, Panchsheel Park, New Delhi - 110 017, India

Penguin Group (NZ), Cnr Airborne and Rosedale Roads, Albany, Auckland 1310, New Zealand
(a division of Pearson New Zealand Ltd)

Penguin Books (South Africa) (Pty) Ltd, 24 Sturdee Avenue,
Rosebank, Johannesburg 2196, South Africa

Registered Offices: Penguin Books Ltd, 80 Strand, London WC2R 0RL, England

First published in the United States of America by Dutton Children's Books,
a division of Penguin Young Readers Group, 2005
Published by Puffin Books, a division of Penguin Young Readers Group, 2006

1 3 5 7 9 10 8 6 4 2

THE LIBRARY OF CONGRESS HAS CATALOGED THE DUTTON EDITION AS FOLLOWS:
Alexander, Lloyd.
The Xanadu adventure/by Lloyd Alexander—1st ed.
p. cm.
Summary: Vesper Holly's adventures continue as she, her guardians, and their friends journey
to Asia Minor in search of the ancient city of Troy, but fall into the trap of an old nemesis.
ISBN 978-0-525-47371-8 (hc)
[1. Adventure and adventurers—Fiction. 2. Turkey—History—Fiction.
3. Troy (Extinct city)—Fiction.] I. Title.
PZ7.A3774Xan   2005
[Fic]—dc22   2004056049

Puffin Books ISBN 978-0-14-240786-8

Designed by Richard Amari
Printed in the United States of America

FOR ADVENTURERS, HOME AT LAST

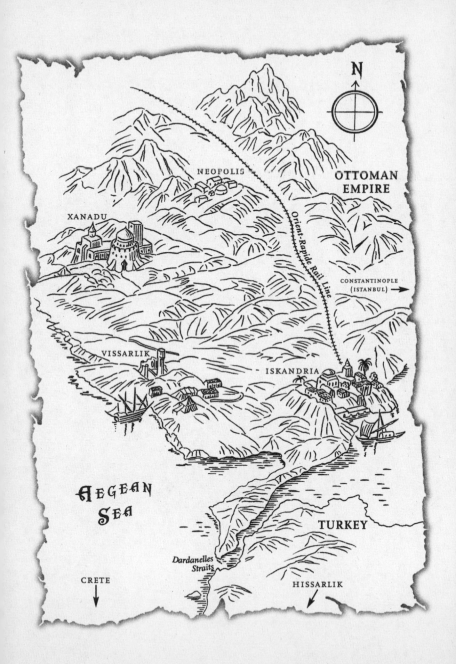

THE
XANADU
ADVENTURE

1

...

MISS VESPER HOLLY leads an active life. In the half-dozen years since my wife, Mary, and I, Professor Brinton Garrett, have been her guardians, I have seen her deal calmly and efficiently with erupting volcanoes, floods, earthquakes, exploding sausages, and other stressful events. The dear girl likes to keep busy.

This autumn of 1876, however, I have become aware that she is neglecting her studies in chemistry, physics, and Renaissance paintings, and seldom plays her banjo. She has, instead, turned the light of her intellect on a single subject: beans.

For that, I hold The Weed responsible. Tobias Wistar Passavant. Vesper has teasingly nicknamed him "The Weed," and a weed indeed he is. He cannot be uprooted: a houseguest who continually says good-bye but never goes away.

He had, months ago, arrived uninvited at Vesper's Strafford mansion near Philadelphia. "Arrived"—I should say:

He happened. Like an epidemic or natural disaster. Vesper graciously allowed him the use of her library to pursue some obscure research in ancient inscriptions. From then on, he was not to be dislodged. There seemed to be a dozen of him. Vesper's estate is large and rambling, but I could hardly turn around without bumping into him. With legs longer than they had any right to be, he looked like a praying mantis; and he ate like a horse. My dear Mary and Vesper herself actually appeared glad to have him in residence. The mental processes of women are, to me, inscrutable.

"Don't grumble, Brinnie," Mary said. "Toby is a perfectly delightful young man."

I was undelighted. I do not wish to speak ill of The Weed. He is, after all, a Philadelphian. Nor do I question his physical courage. This past summer, in fact, he saved Vesper and myself from drowning in the Schuylkill River. I give him that much credit. But, in the process of rescuing us, he severely whacked my head with an oar. I try to keep my distance from him.

I rarely succeed, for he is everywhere at once. His presence makes it impossible for us to stroll uninterrupted through the city. The Weed forever stops to chat with all manner of individuals. He is on a first-name basis with pretzel vendors, horsecar conductors, waiters, shoeshine boys. For all I know, he has acquaintances among prizefighters, baseball players, or worse.

As for the beans:

"It could mean 'lentils,' but most likely 'beans,'" Vesper told me. "It's written in letters nobody can figure out, thousands of years older than ancient Greek. The inscriptions are only in bits and pieces, but if Toby's translation is right, it could be the key to the whole alphabet and a civilization we never knew about."

"That's correct, sir," added The Weed. "We may have ancient history backward. Everybody thinks that Greece spread its culture to Crete and the rest of the Mediterranean. Suppose it was the other way around, and Greek culture came from the Cretans?

"And what about Troy—Ilium, Troia, whatever they called it in those days? In Homer's *Iliad,* Paris runs off with Helen; there's the Trojan War, the wooden horse, and all that. How does Christopher Marlowe put it?" The Weed flung up an arm and declaimed to Vesper, as if she were the only one present:

> *"Was this the face that launch'd a thousand ships,*
> *And burnt the topless towers of Ilium?"*

"Tobias, please," I broke in, for Vesper was blushing, which she seldom does. "There is no need to continue that quotation."

"But, sir, did the Trojan War really happen? Or did Homer make it up?"

"One expects that from poets," I said.

"Toby has a theory," Vesper said.

"I'm sure he does."

We were, that afternoon, in my study. Or what used to be my study. The Weed, like the proverbial camel who poked his nose into the nomad's tent and finally got inside, hump and all, had moved in his notes and transcripts little by little and set up his own worktable. The overflow of his papers threatened to engulf my unfinished history of the Etruscans.

"What I think," said The Weed, "is that Troy was the center of culture for all the Mediterranean. Greeks, Cretans, Romans, even your old Etruscans, sir, learned everything from Troy. The cradle of civilization, you might say."

The Weed had proposed a theory so daring it took my breath away. And there he was, thoroughly tickled with himself; and there was Vesper, green eyes alight, looking at him as if he had just invented the wheel.

"Tobias," I said, "that is no more than a vague hypothesis. Proving it to the satisfaction of the academic world would require years of study, endless work—"

"That's right, sir," The Weed replied. "A bit like your Etruscan history."

"Toby can stay here as long as he wants," Vesper said. "You could give him pointers on doing research."

"Leave it to Carrots to come up with the perfect solution!" The Weed had given Vesper this nickname in retaliation for the one she applied to him; surprisingly, she seemed to enjoy it.

"And what jolly chums we'll be, sir," The Weed rattled on. "You grappling with your Etruscans while I'm swotting away at the Trojans. And Carrots inspiring both of us."

I responded with a mental groan. I envisioned The Weed sharing my study into the distant future, perhaps to the grave and beyond. The prospect of eternity with The Weed did not lift my spirits.

"We'll organize that as soon as we get back," said Vesper.

"Back?" I said. "From where?"

"I told Toby what I had in mind, and he's all for it." Vesper grinned like Moggie, her cat.

"We're going to Troy," she said.

2

...

A_{LL} of us," Vesper hurried on, while The Weed bounced up and down. "You and Aunt Mary. Smiler and Slider—we can't do without them. Toby wanted to go to Crete anyway and look at some inscriptions. If we're that far, we may as well keep going. . . ."

I had always accompanied Vesper on her travels, usually against my better judgment. My solemn obligation to her late father—renowned explorer, scholar, and my old friend— was to offer guidance and the benefit of my experience. Not that she seemed to require it. In this case, my duty was clear.

"Dear girl," I said, "it's not possible. Troy? People have searched for years and never found it. No one knows where it is."

"They do now," said Vesper. "It's in Asia Minor, near the Dardanelles Straits."

"That's right, sir," put in The Weed. "At Hissarlik, just off the Aegean coast. A fellow named Heinrich Schliemann's been digging away at this huge mound. He's sure it's the real site."

My Etruscan studies had so absorbed me that I had to admit I had never heard of him.

"A German chap," said The Weed. "American citizen now. Quite a colorful figure, I gather. Taught himself history, mythology, a dozen languages. Gone all around the world. Started as a poverty-stricken clerk and ended up one of the richest men in Europe. He's paying for the expedition out of his own pocket."

"He's already dug up amazing things," Vesper said. "I keep thinking: What if he found something like the Rosetta stone? That was the key to translating Egyptian hieroglyphics."

I reminded her that one of Napoleon's officers had stumbled on it by lucky accident. I seriously doubted the Trojans had anything similar. To sail off to the wilds of Asia Minor in the vain hope of chancing upon a probably nonexistent inscribed rock?

"Dear girl," I said, "it's a wild-goose chase."

"That's the best kind," said Vesper.

My gentle Mary, to my astonishment, eagerly agreed to Vesper's plan and even wished to press on and visit Constantinople. And so the decision, as with everything Vesper had in mind to do, was out of my hands.

The Weed, however, soon learned that even wild-goose chases present difficulties. To obtain the whole array of permissions and authorizations, he fired off letters to ministries of culture and museum curators. He received no replies. I warned him that scholars and government officials were not famous for answering their mail and moved with glacierlike slowness. I urged patience.

My advice only caused him to haul more documents into my study. Vesper worked side by side with him, her marmalade-colored tresses practically entangled with his tousled mop. With the keen instinct of a devoted guardian, I suspected they might share some small measure of affection.

"Oh, Brinnie, what's the harm?" said Mary when I mentioned this. "Let the young people enjoy each other's company."

"I am not opposed to enjoyment," I said. "I merely suggest that a little of it goes a long way."

Also, I sensed my presence was not necessary. At loose ends, I tried to pass an idle moment with Mrs. Hudson, our admirable housekeeper, but she was too busy for much small talk. I inspected my beehives and fed apples to Hengist and Horsa, Vesper's pair of dappled grays. In the carriage house, I chatted with the twin anchors of our establishment: Smiler and Slider.

Men of their hands, they could rig, repair, and improvise whatever was needed. Their good-natured, weather-beaten faces were so alike I had difficulty telling them apart. Still, I could not escape the presence of The Weed. He always surfaced in our conversations. The twins, to my puzzlement, had only compliments.

"He's a piece of work, is our Mr. Toby." Smiler wagged his head in admiration.

Slider chuckled. "Remember when he kilted himself up like a Malay pirate?"

"And taught us that trick of breathing underwater through a hollow reed?" Smiler added. "Aye, without Mr. Toby we'd have all been goners."

"And rowing like mad up the Schuylkill?" Slider winked at me. "You'll not forget the day, sir."

Not likely. My head ached retrospectively. While Smiler and Slider traded recollections, I hurried inside to commune with Moggie, the cat.

By mid-April, official permissions flooded in. The Weed, galvanized, dashed off to make arrangements.

He took it on himself to book our passage to Athens, then to Crete on a coasting vessel. He hired wagons for our luggage, finished his own packing long before our departure, and spent the remaining days bedeviling us to get ready.

An old traveler, I adopted a more leisurely attitude. I had, that last morning, begun organizing my medical kit when The Weed burst into my quarters, babbling that the wagons had arrived.

"Here, sir, let me give you a hand. We're all downstairs waiting."

Despite my protest, he insisted on helping me—that is to say, he wreaked havoc among my carefully laid-out pharmaceuticals, then snatched away my bags and flung them into one of the vehicles.

We reached the magnificent port of Philadelphia easily with moments to spare. I had not been keen to share a sea voyage with The Weed; but my spirits lifted at a familiar sight: the good ship *City of Brotherly Love*, jewel of our maritime industry. Ladies with parasols, all in their finery, gentlemen in frock coats and top hats, hastened up the companionway. Stewards in spotless white jackets had begun the traditional chant: "All ashore that's going ashore."

Beckoning Smiler and Slider to bring the luggage, I started for the pier. The Weed called me back.

"Not there, sir." He pointed farther down the dockside. "That way."

Vesper and Mary were stepping briskly toward a squat, ungainly freighter belching venomous black smoke from its stacks.

"Tobias!" I cried. "What have you done?"

"I knew you'd like it, sir," The Weed said happily. "I was sure you wouldn't want to be crammed in with a herd of tourists."

He galloped off to join Vesper and Mary. At the rickety gangplank stood a stocky, unshaven fellow in what could pass for a captain's uniform.

"Hello, there, Toby. Glad to have you aboard."

"Hello, there, Fergus," replied The Weed. "Good of you to take us on."

Occupied with nautical duties, Captain Fergus gave us into the charge of a deckhand whose working costume did not include shoes; otherwise, he was an excellent example of a first-class ruffian. He showed us to our staterooms—if they could be so designated. The Weed, Smiler, and Slider were berthed in one cramped cabin; Mary and Vesper in another. I occupied something like a large locker or small closet, with a hammock slung between the bulkheads.

Our first evening at sea, we dined at the captain's table—the only table, but we were the only passengers. Except for The Weed horning in about his translations and the prospect of visiting Hissarlik, the occasion was not unpleasant. Vesper charmed and delighted Captain Fergus with anecdotes of our travels. However, when she came to our final encounter with that archvillain of all time, Dr. Desmond Helvitius, the dear girl was too modest to credit herself with thwarting his scheme to devastate Philadelphia, dominate our United States and the entire Western Hemisphere.

I interrupted to explain that Helvitius had conspired to assassinate our beloved President Grant, the emperor of Brazil, most of the members of Congress, and completely disrupt our glorious Centennial Exposition. Vesper, single-handed, had foiled this murderous plot.

Captain Fergus shook his head in admiration and amazement, but his salt-cured features went grim. "Young lady, you've made yourself a mighty powerful enemy," he said. "I'm no timid sort, but I can tell you this: If I were in your shoes, I'd not sleep easy. Best be on your guard. A villain like that—he's bound to want revenge. He'll come back at you with blood in his eye."

I assured Captain Fergus there was no cause for concern. Thanks to Vesper, Helvitius had joined the choir invisible, assuming it was charitable enough to accept him.

"Oh, Brinnie," put in Mary, "the creature is dead and gone, but we are Philadelphians and should not speak ill of the departed, not even of him."

Vesper turned the conversation to more cheerful topics,

mentioning that once our business in Hissarlik was concluded, we intended traveling on to Constantinople.

"You'll be safe enough in Hissarlik," Captain Fergus said. "It's pretty calm there. But northward, around Constantinople—Istanbul, as Brother Turk calls it—no, not with all that's going on."

Our city's press is the nation's finest in its reportage, but I knew of nothing extraordinary.

"Well, now, I guess you don't," said Captain Fergus. "I only got the news a couple days ago when I put in to refuel. Don't count on that trip, nohow, no way."

Vesper frowned. "Why shouldn't we?"

"Plain and simple," replied Captain Fergus. "There's the very devil of a war.

"It's the Roossians," Captain Fergus went on. "As I hear told, they've got cavalry divisions of wild Cossacks, armies of moujiks or whatever they call them, and heavy artillery, all advancing on Istanbul."

I was not surprised. The Russians and Turks had been at each other's throats for years. In its days of glory, the Ottoman Empire bestrode most of Asia Minor, North Africa, Greece, the Balkans, even to the gates of Vienna. But the sultan's once-mighty realm had been falling into decay. The Russians scented blood.

"The Sool-tahn knows the Russkis got him by the ears," Captain Fergus continued, "but your Ottomans are a ferocious lot of fellows. They'll give a good account of themselves. On the other hand, Brother Russki has the big guns."

"My goodness!" exclaimed Mary. "Are you telling us Istanbul is doomed?"

"Who knows?" Captain Fergus shook his head. "The British will have something to say about it."

"Queen Victoria will take a hand?" replied Mary. "Ah, well, then. I am confident the war will be settled in a dignified fashion."

We dined, each evening of our voyage, with Captain Fergus and his officers. They would excuse themselves to go about ship's business while the rest of us stayed, speculating on the war and talking about new travel plans. I did not linger after dessert but retired to my hammock.

My cubbyhole must have been directly above the engine room. However, by the time we passed through the Straits of Gibraltar into the Mediterranean, I had grown used to the endless pulsation of machinery; it actually lulled me to sleep.

That night, therefore, it took some while for me to become aware of the insistent rapping, and Vesper's voice calling to me.

Still groggy, I forgot I was in a hammock. In my haste, I tipped over and spilled myself onto the deck. I stumbled to open the door. In the dimness, I could barely see Vesper's features.

"Brinnie," she said, "you're my brave old tiger."

"Why—yes, yes," I stammered, fully awake but no less confused.

"So, Brinnie," she went on, "don't be upset and make a fuss."

"Of course not, dear girl. But what—?"

"We're sinking," Vesper said.

3

. . .

TOBY and the twins are in the engine room with Captain Fergus," she added. "I'm going below to have a look. Aunt Mary's on deck. Better stay with her."

She hurried off before I could reply. It was then I realized the engines had fallen ominously silent. I paused only long enough to fling on my dressing gown. I dashed up the companionway. It was just daybreak. I glimpsed Mary at the railing, a traveling cloak about her shoulders. I ran to join her.

"Ah, there you are, Brinnie," she remarked. "I gather the bilges, or scuppers, or some such nautical equipment are not functioning properly. How tiresome. What an inconvenience."

We were, in fact, taking on water fairly rapidly. I stationed myself at Mary's side.

"Steady, my dear." I took her hand. "We must, above all, set an example of how Philadelphians conduct themselves in the face of peril."

In spite of my dressing gown flapping like a loose sail, I

strove to maintain an attitude of calm courage; difficult, for our ship had begun listing appreciably to starboard. The vessel, powerless, was at the mercy of the swelling seas. A sheet of water crashed upon us, tearing loose our grip on the railing. My dear Mary and I went reeling across the deck, where the crew raced to break out cork jackets and rip tarpaulins off the pitifully small lifeboats.

The shrill warbling of a bosun's pipe pierced my ears. The freighter creaked and groaned as if all the bolts and rivets might give way and the hull shatter into pieces. From one moment to the next, I expected to hear the cry that mariners most dread: *Abandon ship!*

Mary had regained her footing beside me. I saw nothing of Vesper, the twins, or The Weed. The horrible realization struck me: They could be trapped below, struggling, drowning in the flooded hold. At all cost, I must find and bring them topside.

"Go, my angel," I said firmly to Mary. "Be ready to take your place in a lifeboat." With as much confidence as I had available, I promised we would soon be with her.

I started running for the companionway. I heard Mary call out to me:

"Brinnie, we are saved!"

I turned for an instant as she pointed seaward. I caught a quick glimpse of a sailing vessel on the horizon. Perhaps Captain Fergus had run up a distress signal sighted by one of the trading craft plying the Mediterranean. It tacked closer, although with agonizing slowness.

I plunged ahead to the companionway, colliding with the

twins climbing topside. They were soaked to the skin, their faces smeared with grease. I did not see Vesper.

I heard the engines throb into life; little by little, our vessel began righting itself. And here was Captain Fergus, wiping his brow with a grimy rag.

"There's a grand pair of fellows," Captain Fergus declared. "Toby, as well. The pumps had quit, and something amiss with the seacocks. Even the chief engineer couldn't figure out why."

By now, with The Weed beside her, Vesper had come on deck. She was as sopping wet as the others, possibly more so.

"But here's the one to credit." Captain Fergus saluted her. "She found the trouble straight off. I'd sign her on as a marine engineer in a jiffy. Aye, without her we'd all be sleeping in Davy Jones's locker."

"Dear girl," I exclaimed in relief, "what an ordeal—"

"I inspected everything belowdecks before we sailed." Captain Fergus scratched his chin. "I don't fathom it."

"Neither do I," said Vesper. "Why did things go wrong? No sign of wear and tear. You'd almost think someone did it on purpose. Which makes no sense."

"Odd, for sure," said Smiler. "Slider and I wondered about that. A murky business any way you look at it. But, no matter. Miss Vesper kept us afloat."

We had, meanwhile, resumed full speed ahead. We went to join Mary at the railing. As best I could observe, the vessel coming to our rescue must have seen we were out of danger, for it veered away and disappeared over the horizon.

Captain Fergus, I am certain, had been resolved to go

down gallantly with his ship. He seemed, nevertheless, relieved that he was not obliged to do so.

"You saved my cargo, my crew, and my neck," he said to Vesper. "Now, my turn to do a little something for you. I'm bound for Athens, but I'll sail you straight to Crete."

Captain Fergus proved as good as his word. Next morning, at Hērákleion harbor, we disembarked with friendly farewells. But The Weed had forgotten to reserve lodgings in advance. We could only haul ourselves and our luggage into town and seek out whatever accommodations were available.

We did, at last, engage several rooms in a hotel a few years younger than the ruins of Knossos. Having escaped drowning, I would have been glad for a nap. The Weed, postponing his work in Crete, wished to go immediately and hire a boat that would take us to Hissarlik.

"Tobias, you will do no such thing," I said, recalling his choice of transportation from Philadelphia. "I shall see to it myself."

"Why, that's very good of you, sir," said The Weed.

I assured him it was my pleasure. Left to his own devices, The Weed might have chartered a canoe.

But not so much as a canoe seemed available. Apparently every craft in Hērákleion harbor had put out to sea. I would have been lucky to find anything that floated.

I continued to the end of the dock, where one remaining boat was moored. It bore the name *Ariadne*. The aroma of deceased fish assaulted me. Nets, tubs, and buckets cluttered the deck. The paint had blistered and peeled, the brightwork was green with tarnish. For all that, *Ariadne* looked a cut above the ordinary: tall-masted, with sleek lines, teakwood decking showing through the grime. Before its presently humble occupation, it had seen happier days.

The captain, wearing a short-visored cap and bearded like a king in Homer's *Iliad,* leaned on the taffrail. I addressed him in Greek, telling him I desired transportation to Hissarlik. He bobbed his head cordially.

"Yaw, yaw," he said.

I went on to explain that my traveling party wished to charter his vessel for a week. I inquired if he had suitable accommodations for six, including two ladies, and asked how much he would charge. He kept smiling and nodding. I paused.

"Sir," I said, "you have not the faintest idea what I'm talking about, do you?"

He answered only with a toothy grin. I switched to Turkish, then Italian and French and received the same yaw-yaw response. I resorted to gestures, with an occasional simple word thrown in, and showed him a handful of money. He brightened remarkably, repeated my gestures, and otherwise made it clear he understood perfectly.

"Tomorrow. Morning." I made motions expressing sunrise.

"Yaw, yaw."

I gave him some coins on account and went back to the hotel, feeling pleased with my accomplishment. Mary had stored most of our luggage with the proprietor. Vesper, expert at traveling lightly, had already packed; the twins likewise. The Weed still dithered, trying to decide what to take and what to leave. All were delighted by my success. I urged them to retire early for a good night's sleep. Which we did, except for The Weed popping in and out to make sure we were ready.

At dawn, after a quick breakfast, we made our way to the dockside. Captain Yaw-Yaw—I had no better name for him—awaited us as agreed. He beckoned us aboard *Ariadne*, where the fishy aroma had ripened overnight. He ushered us into what once might have been the master's cabin, fairly spacious but now crammed with coils of rope and piles of nets. He indicated we all were to reside there. Dismayed, I protested and made signs that we desired additional quarters. He gave a couple of yaw-yaws and left us where we stood.

I wholeheartedly—and a little sheepishly—apologized for the lack of comforts. Mary, undaunted, prepared a burrow of netting. The twins, used to roughing it, sat with their backs to the bulkhead. The Weed poked about here and there. Vesper, usually uncomplaining, put a hand on my arm.

"Brinnie," she said for my ears alone, "I don't like this. It makes my flesh creep."

"Mine, too, dear girl," I said. "It's the fish."

"No. Something else." Vesper glanced around the cabin. "I've been here before. So have you."

4

...

$DEAR$ girl," I answered, "that's not possible."

"It is," she insisted. "I can't put my finger on it, but it bothers me."

Vesper looked as deeply concerned as I had ever seen her.

"It's different," she murmured, "but the same."

"Very simple," I explained. "What you are sensing is merely the false impression of repeating something that previously happened. As the French so neatly put it—déjà vu."

"Yes," Vesper said. "Déjà vu. Literally."

"And there you have it," I said. "Only a harmless illusion."

"If I think I've been here before," Vesper said, "it's because I have. Brinnie, don't you remember? Persian carpets. Paintings." Vesper waved a hand around the cabin. "A desk and chairs. A globe in a wooden frame—"

Of course, The Weed had to come and horn in. "What's wrong, Carrots?"

Vesper repeated her description of the furnishings. Something disagreeable tugged at my memory.

"A picture hung there," she went on. "And another one. See the pale spaces where they used to be? What about that?"

I suggested, lamely, careless housecleaning. The dear girl was upsetting me more and more.

"We're not aboard *Ariadne*," she said.

"Of course we are," I said. "Where else?"

"*Minotaur*."

The name sent a chill through me. I had struggled to blot the whole horrible episode from my memory. I could no longer do so. Vesper was right, beyond my attempts at denial.

Yes, it had been that luxurious yacht; and, in this very cabin, Helvitius had held us captive.

"Why change the name?" asked The Weed.

"I don't know," Vesper said. "Not yet, anyway. I'm going on deck. I want a little talk with the captain."

She had no need to seek him out; for, a moment later, in he came bearing a tray of midmorning refreshments.

Vesper stepped up to him. "This is really *Minotaur*, isn't it?"

"Yaw, yaw." He gave his usual cheery smile.

Vesper, frankly and directly, asked how he had come into possession of the vessel, when, and in what circumstances.

"Yaw, yaw," he said.

Few can withstand Vesper's polite though incisive questioning. But, no matter how she pressed, she got nothing more from him.

"I'm starting to wonder," Vesper said, after Captain Yaw-Yaw clambered topside, "does he know more than he lets on?" She folded her arms and stood silent for a few moments. "There's something odd about all this. It also makes me wonder—what if Helvitius is alive?"

"Not the remotest chance in the world," I quickly assured her. "Banish such a thought, put your mind at ease. As you recall, our police force, Philadelphia's finest, combed every inch of the area, dragged the whole length of the river, and found nothing. A brigade of our shrewdest detectives analyzed the case in microscopic detail. They unanimously concluded he had been swept out to sea and perished.

"One final proof, as if more were needed," I went on, "you well know Helvitius treasured *Minotaur*. Alive, he would never have let it slip from his clutches."

For the rest, I explained, the United States Navy had seized the yacht. Such confiscated vessels were usually sold at auction, and, by some chain of events, it had eventually come into the hands of Captain Yaw-Yaw. He, or a prior purchaser, had changed the name. The once-elegant craft had been reduced to a fishing boat.

"It is, dear girl," I said, "no more than a bizarre coincidence, an ironic twist of fate."

"Possible," Vesper said, not altogether satisfied. "If that's true, it's a sorry end for *Minotaur*."

"What does Hamlet say to Horatio in the graveyard?" The Weed put in:

> *"Imperious Caesar, dead and turned to clay,*
> *Might stop a hole to keep the wind away:*
> *O, that that earth, which kept the world in awe,*
> *Should patch a wall to expel the winter's flaw!"*

"Mr. Toby," said Smiler, as Slider nodded agreement, "it's an education to hear you expostulate."

I held my head.

I felt sure my analysis was correct, and found nothing to suggest otherwise. Though our quarters were uncomfortable and odoriferous, Captain Yaw-Yaw proved himself attentive to all our needs to the best of his abilities and resources. He made it clear that he welcomed our presence on deck; we gladly accepted his invitation to enjoy the fresh salt air.

Vesper, however, seemed pensive, no doubt recalling our captivity on this selfsame vessel. The Weed grew only bouncier:

"Can't you just imagine, sir, we're part of the Greek fleet heading for Troy? Painted sails bellying in the wind—"

I told him I had difficulty relating the Greek armada to our present mode of transportation. Even so, *Ariadne* was making splendid headway, scudding over the waves as if regaining former grandeur, skimming past the islands dotting the Aegean—there must have been hundreds of them, as if Zeus had flung down fistfuls of Olympian-sized gravel. Indeed, many were hardly bigger than large rocks, with some green patches, and white, pink-roofed houses clinging like barnacles to the slopes.

"You know, sir," The Weed maundered on, "come right down to it, I can't help feeling sorry for Hector, Andromache, old King Priam, and the terrible things that happened to them."

Leave it to The Weed to take the Trojan side. "Tobias," I

said, "King Menelaus was the aggrieved party. Paris, after all, ran off with his wife."

"Yes, as Homer tells it," The Weed admitted. "But suppose it was really just a trade war. A power struggle, like the Russians going at it with the Turks?"

Whatever it had been, I told him, it was thousands of years ago, long over and done. I was glad when dinner was served. Then sorry. It gave me indigestion, and I slept badly that night.

The underdone fish swimming in a sea of olive oil probably set it off, but Helvitius loomed large in my thoughts: the shock of white hair, the false, blood-chilling smile. Worse, the creature's overbearing arrogance—apart from being a ruthless killer. Vesper and I had encountered him in Illyria, where he claimed to be a historian. His attempt to annihilate us with dynamite bombs raised serious doubts regarding his character. I had never trusted him since.

We made landfall the next morning and prepared to disembark: Mary in a fashionable travel costume; the twins in workman's garb. Vesper and I wore our usual and very practical canvas knickerbockers. The Weed had somewhere acquired high socks and a pair of sand-colored short trousers like two stovepipes barely reaching his excessively knobby knees. He was first to leap off *Ariadne* when we tied up at the narrow little pier.

The rest of us followed at a more deliberate pace. I lingered behind a moment to confirm our arrangements: We would sleep ashore—bad enough to be herded into that stifling cabin during the return voyage—while *Ariadne* awaited us at dockside. Our shipboard host gave his invariable reply:

"Yaw, yaw," he said.

The Weed, flinging himself about, gestured toward the wide apron of sand on either side of the harbor:

"Look there, sir. That's where the Greek army would have camped, with all their ships riding at anchor just offshore."

I must have been in a weakened, suggestible state of mind in consequence of a restless night and the hot land breeze from Asia Minor; for, in this case, I agreed with him. I could easily envision the Greek encampment crowding the beach; and one tent perhaps set a little aloof, where sulked wrathful Achilles, peeved that he had not been given a captured maiden and a larger share of plunder; and, farther inland, where he boastfully dragged the desecrated body of noble Hector. As I came to think on it again, The Weed had a point. The Greek invaders were hardly a charming group.

The famous walls and topless towers, of course, were long gone. I did see a large mound showing signs of excavation. Vesper was making her way in that direction. The Weed and I followed—I, lagging a few paces behind. The wind weighed on me like a heavy hand; I was already perspiring.

Vesper had reached the site of the dig, which was neatly staked out, with lengths of cords crisscrossing into a grid. A crew of workmen shoveled and sifted the crumbling earth. Their efforts were overseen by a short, dumpy figure in riding breeches and boots, a cork sun helmet crammed onto his head.

No sooner aware of Vesper's presence than he approached—in some vexation, I thought. He had a round, fleshy face with an aggressive mustache. He did not remove his sun helmet.

Vesper, with her unfailing graciousness, extended a hand: "Herr Schliemann, I presume?"

The man took a backward step, as if her courteously offered hand had struck him in the face. His lips twitched, his mustache did gymnastics.

"I assure you," he retorted, "I most certainly am not."

5

. . .

"IN that case," Vesper said pleasantly, despite this individual's churlish attitude, "can you tell us where to find Herr Schliemann?"

"Speak not that name!" the man flung back. "It is offensive to my ears. How dare you interrogate me regarding that—that person?"

Vesper maintained a cordial air in the face of his outburst. "I'm only asking if you know where he is."

"Explain, first, your business with that bumbling incompetent," the man countered. "An archaeologist? Careless dirt-grubber! He destroys all he digs up. An obsessive monomaniac! Does he think himself a scholar? He has no grasp of his subject, he could not pass the most elementary examination—"

Since he was carrying on so, I naturally assumed he and Herr Schliemann were colleagues, and I said as much.

"Colleagues?" he burst out. "Never! Ill educated—no, uneducated. He has not an hour of higher learning, no advanced degree—the ignoramus barely graduated from kindergarten.

What are his credentials, certifications, diplomas? Money. He presumes his fortune can buy admission to the noble groves of academe. Are you aware of the source of his tawdry gains? Profiteering in the Crimean War, selling dyestuffs to the Russian army, and whatever else he could do to turn a penny. No better than a common tradesman, a grocery clerk, as in fact he was at the start of his career."

I took this at first as the usual rancor found in the rough-and-tumble academic world; but his ranting went beyond the normal institutional slander.

"We were told," said Vesper, trying to introduce a soothing note, "that Herr Schliemann"—the man winced at the name—"is at Hissarlik."

"And so he is. Therefore, he is not here. Simple logic."

Vesper frowned. "But where—?"

"You are not at Hissarlik. You are in Vissarlik."

"Captain Yaw-Yaw! Captain Idiot!" I could have throttled that fool of a navigator. I had told him our destination; the dunderhead had brought us here instead.

Our interlocutor folded his arms and eyed us as if we were a classroom of dunces.

"There are two distinct areas," he said. "Hissarlik is on the other side of the straits."

"It's all right, Brinnie," said Vesper. "That's hardly any distance at all. *Ariadne* can sail us there in no time.

"Sorry we bothered you," Vesper said to our instructor in geography. "Before we go, would you be kind enough to tell us whom we've had the pleasure of addressing?"

"I am," he declared, elevating his tone and chin, "Professor-Doctor Mirko Dionescu."

"Nice to have met . . . " Vesper hesitated. "Dionescu, you said?"

"Formerly of the classical studies department," he replied, "at the University of Cludj."

I drew in my breath, as we all did upon hearing the name of this venerable, world-renowned institution of higher learning.

"Then," Vesper said, "can you be the same Mirko Dionescu, the author?"

"Can be. And am. Do you imply familiarity with my *Short Dictionary of Classical Antiquities?*"

We murmured, awestruck. His massive, three-volume magnum opus held a place of honor on the shelf of every classical scholar.

When Vesper revealed that she had pored over this compilation, the effect was nothing short of miraculous.

Professor Dionescu's features turned instantly radiant, color bloomed on his cheeks, his mustache relaxed. He was, before our very eyes, transformed into a model of benevolence. Vesper presented us, emphasizing my own professorial title.

"Let me take this unexpected pleasure and opportunity," I said. "A word with you, sir, regarding your coverage of the Etruscans."

"Your field of expertise?" Professor Dionescu raised an eyebrow. "I confess I have not read your work on the subject."

I replied that my history remained as yet unfinished. He gave me the disdainful, walleyed stare that one academic bestows on another. I judged it best not to question him further; but then The Weed had to step in.

"Your latest publications, sir? We're all eager to read them. Can you give us the titles?"

"Ah." Dionescu's mustache trembled, his radiance dimmed. "With the exception of an occasional featured article in the more prestigious Serbo-Croatian journals—no, I have been much too preoccupied." He indicated the excavations taking place around us. "This absorbs my every waking moment."

Vesper congratulated him on being in charge of such an extensive site. She assured him she understood why it took precedence over generating further publications.

"Once my work is complete," he said, "you may be certain my findings will be revealed to the entire world."

"Adding to your laurels, sir," The Weed said, which restored much of Dionescu's glow.

"And, as well," I said, "redounding to the credit of the University of Cludj. I assume your endeavors are being carried out under the aegis of that noble institution."

"No," he snapped. "No, sir, they are not. My investigations are conducted privately. I am not obliged to justify my expenditures to dull-witted reviewing boards and penny-pinching accounting departments."

Vesper glanced around the site. "This takes a lot of pennies."

"Worth every one of them," Dionescu replied. "What I have discovered—"

He broke off as Mary and the twins came running toward us.

"Miss Vesper," Smiler called out, "*Ariadne*'s left us here. She's put out to sea."

CHAPTER

6

...

To calm the agitated Smiler, I assured him he was mistaken. I had made it absolutely clear that the vessel was to wait for us. Captain Yaw-Yaw was merely seeking a better anchorage.

Smiler pointed beyond the harbor. "I wouldn't call that anchoring."

"More like hightailing it out of here," said Slider.

Ariadne was, in fact, cutting with all possible speed through the waves.

"Damn Captain Yaw-Yaw!" I shook my fist at the rapidly disappearing figure at the helm.

"Hush, Brinnie." Mary nudged my arm. "There is no need for profanity."

"Damn him anyway!" I cried. "He's marooned us!"

"I'm sure he has not," Mary said. "He knows his services are not immediately required. He sees no point wasting time in idleness when he could be pursuing his fishing activities. I commend his diligence. His absence is only temporary."

My dear Mary finds goodness in everyone. Her explanation was generous-hearted, sweetly reasonable. And wrong. At the rate he was skipping along, Captain Yaw-Yaw would be past returning at any time in the foreseeable future.

Vesper understood the hard truth of the matter.

"He's gone for keeps," she said.

"After him!" I exclaimed. "Is there nothing in the harbor that can overtake the wretch?"

The twins shook their heads. "No," said Smiler.

"Not so much as a raft," added Slider.

I turned away in despair. We were, for all practical purposes, castaways.

Professor Dionescu stepped forward. "Miss Holly, do not be distressed. I understand that you have been inconvenienced, but it is only a small contretemps. A packet boat is due to arrive from Athens with provisions. It will, I am sure, transport you wherever you wish."

"When?" said Vesper.

"In this part of the world, shipping schedules are, shall we say, flexible," Dionescu replied. "I would estimate within the next ten days; at most, two weeks."

Vesper had to accept our situation, but I saw she did not find it much to her liking. She explained our urgent business regarding the mysterious script The Weed was attempting to decipher; and, as expected, The Weed broke in to babble about vowel frequencies, recurring suffixes, and would have rambled on forever had I not encouraged him to stop.

Professor Dionescu appeared greatly interested. "It is possible, as one colleague to another, I may be able to help you. It would, however, require a certain amount of time."

"Jolly decent of you," The Weed replied. "I'd be glad—"

"Please, please, Tobias," I said. "We appreciate the offer, all the more since it comes from a distinguished academic. But we have difficulties more urgent than beans. First, where and how do we live for the next couple of weeks?"

"I offer you my hospitality, such as it is," said Dionescu, "and you are most welcome. You shall stay here at the site."

Except for The Weed, who seized on the invitation immediately, we murmured the refusals that courtesy requires.

"No, no, I insist upon it. You shall be my guests," Dionescu said. "Come, take some refreshment while I arrange your accommodations."

He beckoned for us to follow him to the open front of a large, four-walled tent near the excavation. He bustled around eagerly unfolding canvas camp chairs and summoned a couple of his crew to prepare trays. He also instructed his foreman to pitch several tents for our exclusive use.

Though a scholar of the highest distinction, Dionescu could not have been more attentive to our comforts. True, during our exchange of small talk, I did let slip—yes, deliberately—that Vesper was the daughter of the eminent Dr. Benjamin Rittenhouse Holly. Which, I believe, carried added weight with him.

"It's not just the inscriptions," Vesper said as we sat at our ease. "Toby has a theory. He needs to go to Hissarlik and have a look at Herr Schliemann's excavation of Troy—"

"Troy?" Dionescu exploded. "That charlatan! That fraud! That individual is a fool, a liar, or both. Do you seek Troy? You are there already."

Vesper gave him a questioning look, but withheld any comment. Dionescu hurried on:

"As I was about to reveal when you first arrived . . ."

He paused for dramatic effect, an old professorial trick.

"Ancient Ilium, the glorious Troy of the *Iliad,* lies beneath your feet," he declared. "I have discovered the true site."

"What about Hissarlik?" said Vesper.

"Hissarlik?" Dionescu retorted. "A deception foisted on the academic world by that self-deluded guttersnipe! That jumped-up grocery boy! No, no, it is in Vissarlik. You were brought to this place by a misunderstanding, but a most fortunate one. Troy is precisely here."

Dionescu, then and there, insisted on our inspecting the diggings. I would rather have stayed behind to recuperate from the shock of being marooned. Vesper, always curious, could not resist; nor could The Weed, especially after Dionescu's thunderbolt announcement. So, nothing for it, I had to tag behind Mary and the twins. Armed with a riding crop serving as a blackboard pointer, and bursting with pride, Dionescu indicated the areas he expected soon to uncover.

"I have closely studied ancient architecture," he told us. "Geology, as well—essential when dealing with strata and substrata. By my calculations, the famous walls would have enclosed this perimeter." He waved the crop in a great circle, then turned to the network of cords. "Here, the royal palace. Here, the forecourt, the interior hallways—"

"Why, that could be the very spot where Pyrrhus killed old King Priam." The Weed was off and running again. "'The rugged Pyrrhus . . . trick'd with blood of fathers, mothers, daughters, sons . . .' How does the line in *Hamlet* go, sir? With Queen Hecuba wrapped in a blanket and rags around her head instead of a crown? The palace in flames, the Trojans all put to the sword—"

"Tobias," I said, "we agree the slaughter was brutal. I suggest to you that Shakespeare, certainly not present at the scene, may have overdrawn the picture." I reminded him that a good many Trojans escaped. According to Virgil, Aeneas led them to Africa—that scandalous affair with Queen Dido—and on to Italy.

"That's right," said Vesper. "For all we know, others may have gotten away, too, and scattered over Asia Minor."

The dear girl, with her usual keen insight, had offered a fascinating speculation, but I was feeling too peaky to pursue it. Dionescu herded us along on his guided tour. He kept at it until nearly dusk.

"This is not the only site of interest," he said. "There is yet another, absolutely extraordinary. Truly unique. I know of nothing like it.

"You, Mr. Passavant," he went on, turning to The Weed, "should find a visit there most profitable. I believe you will discover valuable clues to your translations. The site is not far. I estimate less than a day's travel up-country."

The Weed, of course, wanted to set out instantly. Dionescu sensibly advised waiting until morning.

"It will be a short excursion," he said. "There is no need to overburden yourselves. Take only the barest essentials. My stores can provide sufficient food and water."

"We shall return long before the packet boat arrives," Dionescu assured us. "Meantime, it is an opportunity not to be missed."

He led us back to his tent, where dinner was being prepared. The Weed was jumping out of his skin with impatience, which did not affect his appetite. Vesper, Mary, and the twins were likewise eager. I did not finish my meal and begged to be excused.

Several canvas pyramids had been pitched during our absence. Dionescu pointed out the one Mary and I were to occupy. I was glad to crawl into it. The night chill, which sets in so quickly after sundown, had seeped into my bones. I flung myself onto a thin pallet and fell asleep instantly.

Mary shook me awake. She had already packed our bags. Frankly, I muttered, I was not overwhelmingly interested in the excursion. I did not mention my nagging headache, since I did not wish to worry her.

My joints creaked in protest as I dressed and crawled from the tent. Everyone else looked hale and hearty: the twins, with rucksacks on their shoulders and bandannas around their heads; Vesper, bright-eyed, chatting with The Weed; and Dionescu, displaying professorial eagerness to lead us on our way.

And so, set off we did. Dionescu had provided two donkeys for the ladies, but Vesper preferred going on foot beside The Weed. Mary declined to burden her rawboned animal and strode along vigorously. As a point of pride, I, too, would have walked. But after we crossed the scraggle of the lowlands and entered the foothills, I was grateful to climb aboard an unoccupied donkey. The air freshened as we gained the higher ground, which I found to be a great relief. However, I became aware of two things.

First, Dionescu had no sense of time, distance, or terrain. What he led us to believe would be a short hike proved otherwise. Noon was long past. By his own admission, we had only gone halfway.

Second, I became ill, and sicker with every jolting step. I blamed myself. I should have recognized the warning symptoms. My ailment was a cousin—a vicious, virulent cousin—of breakbone fever. I had acquired it when Vesper's father and I visited Benares to observe the funeral pyres, the famous ghats on the banks of India's legendary River Ganges. We chose to take a cleansing dip in the mystical waters. I emerged hopefully purified in spirit but with the physical agonies of what is vulgarly called "Shiva's Revenge."

It came upon me from time to time, never especially troublesome, never hampering my journeys with Vesper; for I had, long ago, obtained an effective remedy. If only I had taken it before now. The heavy, debilitating winds of Asia Minor had no doubt brought it on. But that was beside the point. The sum and substance: I could go no farther.

The fever was rampaging through my limbs. I was giddy with pain. The twins lifted me from the donkey and let me lie on a stretch of turf. I pleaded to return to Dionescu's camp.

To my surprise and dismay, Dionescu grew close to peevish. He argued it would take as long to go back to the seacoast as it would to press on to our destination. I was too sick to debate with him. I barely had strength to ask Mary if she had brought my medical kit.

"Of course, dear Brinnie," she said. "I know you never travel without it."

"Angel of mercy!" I gasped. "The brown flask. You cannot mistake it."

She was back in what seemed an hour but was surely only a few moments.

"Brinnie," she said, "I find nothing like it. Are you certain you packed it?"

I groaned. The Weed! Even in my feverish state, I remembered, with crystal clarity, the morning The Weed had come to hurry me along, disordering my carefully arranged medicines. In the eye of memory, I clearly saw the flask sitting on the dresser. Distracted by The Weed, I had left it there.

I slid into unconsciousness. When I opened my eyes again, I met the critical gaze of a large billy goat.

7

. . .

WHY am I in Illyria?" I murmured in that first alarming moment before the fog cleared from my head. I realized then that my mind had flown me back to an old face-to-face encounter with Illyrian goats. This one apparently was a resident, along with some chickens I heard clucking around me. I sat up from a straw mattress. Here were Vesper and Mary beside me, watching with relief. The room itself was much like others throughout the Aegean—pleasantly airy, with white plaster walls. The lady of the house, a kerchief on her head and wearing an embroidered vest, was nodding and smiling. I smiled back. I had no idea where I was.

"What a turn you gave us, Brinnie." Mary laid a hand on my forehead. "But all's well. You're going to be fine."

"We can thank Smiler and Slider," Vesper added.

"So we can, sir," The Weed spoke up. "Yesterday, we were a bit like Buridan's ass between two equally attractive bales of hay. You know the old philosophical problem. A logical dilemma. How could he decide which one to choose? Or did he starve to death trying to make up his mind?"

Yes, The Weed was there, gawking behind Vesper. Now it fell into place. Shiva's Revenge, my medicine left at home. Oddly enough, I was in such good spirits that I said not a word of reproach to him. I had benevolent feelings toward the world at large, including the goat.

The twins, meantime, had come forward to have a look at me.

"What it was, sir," began Smiler, "after you temporarily left us, as it were, that professor chap was fussing as how we should sling you over a donkey and keep on our way."

"Miss Vesper was flat against that," Slider said. "She wanted to take you back to the seacoast—but she was worried you couldn't stand the trip."

"So we thought we'd just have a walkabout while they were arguing," said Smiler. "Sure enough, it didn't take us long. We found a young lad with a herd of goats."

"He couldn't understand a word of what we were telling him," Slider added. "Nor we couldn't understand him any way at all."

I groaned. "Not another Captain Yaw-Yaw."

"No," said Vesper. "You're in for a surprise."

"Anyhow," Slider said, "we got him to follow us—the professor was still fussing—and that bright lad saw right off you were in trouble. He told Miss Vesper his village was close by, they had a doctor who'd set you right in no time."

"Miss Vesper did pretty well, gabbling away with him," Smiler put in. "And so, sir, here you are, looking good as new after that doctor fellow poured some sort of concoction down your throat."

It must have been a powerful dose. I could still feel it bubbling happily through my system. I glanced around. I did not see Dionescu. I asked where he was.

"Something like Buridan's ass," Vesper said. "Betwixt and between. On the one hand, he wasn't pleased when we turned off and took you here; he's still fidgeting to be on our way again. On the other, he's met some of the village elders, he's seen a few things, and can't tear himself away."

"Really amazing, sir," The Weed added. "You'll come have a look for yourself."

Despite my sense of well-being, I was not eager to rejoin Dionescu since learning that he would have slung me across a donkey's back—crude, even for an academic. Still, The Weed roused my curiosity. I made an effort to stand up.

"You'll go after the *chiron* sees you," Vesper said.

"Who?" I asked. The only Chiron I could think of was the mythological old centaur. After so many strange turns of events, I would not have been overly astonished to see a half-man, half-horse come trotting up.

"The *chiron*," Vesper said. "This is his house. *Chiron* is their word here for a doctor. But Chiron the centaur was a sort of doctor, too; he knew all about healing herbs, plants, roots . . ."

It was interesting, I told her, that such a name had persisted. I wondered how these village folk had picked it up.

"What's more interesting," Vesper said, "is that they speak Greek."

"I expect they would," I answered. It was hardly an uncommon language in this part of the world.

"Not just Greek," Vesper said. "Classical Greek. Ancient Greek! Brinnie, it's as if we went to some town lost in the Drexel Hills back home and found everybody speaking Old English.

"It's not perfect," she went on. "There's some Turkish mixed in with it and who knows what else. They call their marketplace *egerun*—that's *agora* in Greek. The village chief's the *vassilos*, nearly the same as Greek *basileus*, the word for 'king.'"

Vesper began detailing a few more words and fragments. "It's like pieces of broken pottery," she said. "By themselves, they're just rubbish. Put them together, they turn out to be an ancient Greek wine jar—"

She stopped, for here came the *chiron* himself, a hale old fellow in something like a nightshirt tied around his waist with braided cords. His full head of hair, and his beard in curls, gave him a striking resemblance to the bust of Herodotus in my study.

"*Khaire*," he greeted me. Then, in the way of physicians no doubt since the days of Hippocrates, he thumped my chest and peered down my throat and up my nose, all the while muttering "Hmm" and "Aha." Nodding in satisfaction, he told me I was fine, that I should get up and move around, the exercise would do me good.

I had some difficulty understanding him, but Vesper was right: Along with infusions of Turkish, there were shadows and echoes of ancient Greek behind his words. I thanked him profusely and asked about the remarkable medication he had given me. He only smiled mysteriously, which I took to mean it was a professional secret. He did promise to give me a pouch of the dry ingredients, which I could steep in water if needed. All in all, he was as brisk and efficient as any Philadelphia specialist.

The *chiron* went off on his rounds. Following his advice, I did get up. Sure now I was completely well, Mary and the twins turned their attention to the clever design of the oven and vented cookstove, and the various implements of what the *chiron*'s wife called the *oikos*, recognizably Greek for "household."

Vesper, still keeping a concerned eye on me, led me from the house. The Weed was already loping down the wide stretch of gravel, doubtless the main street of the village. As soon as they caught sight of him, half a dozen youngsters left off their games to skip after him. I had no idea what so attracted them, unless it was that he had the longest, boniest shanks of any individual they had ever seen.

The Weed, to say this much for him, took it in good spirits. He actually scooped up one of the small girls and set her on his shoulder. With the others, he performed that tired old trick of pretending to catch their noses between his fingers and made them whoop and giggle as if he had done some sort of miracle. He laughed as much as they did, with no sense of adult dignity, and generally made a fool of himself. Vesper, however, beamed at him.

Mary and the twins caught up with us as we reached the largest building, which I took to be the equivalent of our City

Hall, though of course smaller and plainer than Philadelphia's noble edifice. Dionescu was there at a wooden table among what I assumed were village elders, perhaps the municipal council. I gave him only a nod of minimum civility; his suggestion of flinging me like a sack of grain on a jackass continued to rankle. He did not inquire about my health, nor did I inquire about his. In any case, he was entirely absorbed in conversation with the authorities.

"I showed them copies of my inscriptions," The Weed explained. "They got really excited. They're friendly chaps, glad to help us any way they can."

"*Khaire,* Toby." The *vassilos,* the village chief, a wiry old man with a mustache like bicycle handlebars, greeted The Weed as if they were the best of chums. He invited us to look at an array of clay tablets.

"See the letters on them, sir," The Weed said. "They're the same as mine."

The *vassilos* began speaking so rapidly I could barely keep up with his remarks. I did get the general drift. The tablets had been treasured up as venerable objects. It would take some days of study to decipher The Weed's inscriptions, but the *vassilos* was sure it could be done.

"There's something else," Vesper said to me. "The name of the village: Neopolis—'new city.' These folk have old songs and stories about invaders from the sea, and a great fire ages ago."

"It sounds like the Trojan War, sir, wouldn't you say?" The Weed put in. "They still remember it after—what—thousands of years."

I agreed. Having one's city invaded and burned would tend to stick in the memory.

"Which can mean," said Vesper, "their ancestors were Trojan refugees."

The *vassilos* assured us we were welcome to stay as long as we pleased. His colleagues, something like a local Chamber of Commerce, smiled proudly and nodded agreement. They all appeared sincerely delighted by our interest. As for Dionescu, I saw that he was torn between wanting to stay and wanting to go. His eyes lit up at the sight of the artifacts. Still, he fidgeted and kept muttering we should be on our way.

Vesper and The Weed, I am sure, would have accepted the invitation to remain for days on end. I raised the question of the packet boat.

Vesper shrugged this off. "It's like horsecars. Miss one, there's always another."

Dionescu resolved the dilemma. We were not far from our destination, he told us. If we left now, we could be there before nightfall, camp at the site, and be back at the village two days later. The Weed's inscriptions would be deciphered; if not, we would wait until they were. He himself was most eager to examine the village archives and artifacts.

Vesper and The Weed agreed with his plan. I had to admit it made sense. I hurried to find the *chiron* and obtain more of his excellent concoction. We packed hastily, leaving nearly all our gear in the good hands of the *chiron*'s wife. The village youngsters trooped after us, waving and calling to The Weed.

Though feeling completely well, I climbed aboard one of

the donkeys at Mary's insistence. I did comment to Dionescu that I preferred riding astride to being flung over the creature's back. My barbed remark went unnoticed.

Dionescu, this time, got his bearings right. We made our way briskly through the foothills to a wide, level expanse. Well before sundown, we halted at the site. I confess I was astonished.

I had expected ruined columns, shattered arcades, the toppled portico of a once-stately structure. But the edifice stood in perfect condition, and was the strangest I had ever seen. It had a dome to match any in Istanbul; a couple of slender towers, like minarets; buttressed walls; iron-latticed balconies. The main entry was in the Imperial Chinese style. It could have been the dream of some deranged architect.

Dionescu was delighted to see us staring open-mouthed in wonder. He led us to the heavy portal. I glimpsed some sheds and outbuildings; and workmen, no doubt an archaeological crew, trundling wheelbarrows and otherwise going about their business.

To my added astonishment, the building was inhabited. Dionescu must have been a familiar visitor, for a manservant in Turkish garb beckoned him inside with many salaams and courteous gestures to all of us.

We followed down a high-ceilinged corridor decorated with tiles and mosaics—museum pieces, all of them.

"Brinnie," murmured Vesper, pointing to rows of glowing fixtures, "they have gaslight here."

I had no time to contemplate those modern appointments, for we were ushered into a softly illuminated chamber that looked like the interior of a sheik's tent. Great swags of silken draperies hung all around. Rich carpets covered the floor and walls. On a low divan, a figure wearing a jeweled turban and billowing pantaloons lounged amid a pile of embroidered cushions.

At sight of us, he made no effort to rise but merely waved a hand glittering with precious stones.

"Welcome to Xanadu," said Dr. Helvitius.

8

...

UNTIL this instant, I had assumed—no, I had been certain beyond the shadow of a doubt—that Helvitius had found a watery grave, perhaps off the shores of Atlantic City. But here he was before my eyes, in solid flesh, in full health and vigor. I was disappointed to see him looking so well.

Vesper always keeps her composure in the most horrendous circumstances. Though I knew she was as shocked as all of us, she held her unwavering gaze on Helvitius. For once, however, the sight of him left her momentarily speechless. Understandably. Coming face to face in the backlands of Asia Minor with someone long dead is bound to produce awkward moments.

Helvitius obviously relished our discomfort. He leaned back on his divan, nodded cordially to each of us, then returned his glance to Vesper.

"My dear Miss Holly," he said, with nauseating satisfaction, "you look as if you have seen a ghost."

"Too bad you aren't," Vesper said.

The Weed, that lunatic, started forward as if to fling himself at Helvitius; Smiler and Slider gave signs of boldly supporting his assault. But Helvitius raised a hand; his eyes went toward the rear of the chamber. I turned to see four or five burly ruffians. All bore gleaming scimitars thrust into their crimson waistbands.

"Mr. Passavant, I urge you to forgo pointless heroics," Helvitius said pleasantly. "The fearsome blades you see are ornamental. For serious work, these gentlemen prefer modern weapons. They are equipped with excellent Colt revolvers.

"Pray be seated, put yourselves at ease." Helvitius indicated the oversize pillows strewn about the floor. "Calm your minds. You are, naturally, bewildered, wondering how it was possible for me to have survived those fatal events in your native city—"

"I'm not really interested in the details," Vesper said.

"Come, come, Miss Holly, I cannot believe that," said Helvitius. "With your insatiable curiosity you are surely dying—I use the word 'dying' in its most exact and literal sense—to know how I accomplished the impossible."

Not only had he trapped us, the scoundrel was, as well, determined to gloat. Vesper shrugged and sat down on one of the cushions. We followed her example. What else could we do? We were tired; it was late in the day. Yet I knew her mind was racing at top speed, analyzing every avenue of escape.

"So," said Vesper, "you mean to bore us to death."

"Not in the least, Miss Holly." Helvitius took no offense at her comment. I had never seen him in better spirits. "You will find it intriguing. Simple, but intriguing in its simplicity.

"I am a strong swimmer, with exceptional pulmonary capacity," he continued. "I swam underwater and emerged farther downriver, where I climbed easily ashore. Your City of Brotherly Love has an unrivaled system of public transportation; thus, I boarded a horsecar that carried me close to my destination: a haven among certain individuals who provided accommodations and secrecy.

"*Minotaur* had been seized; but, thanks to the influence of highly placed persons—let them be nameless—the vessel was released from impound. My agents bought it for a pittance, and I regained possession. It suited my purposes to disguise the craft as a fishing boat. I renamed it *Ariadne*—"

"Captain Yaw-Yaw!" I burst out. "One of your creatures! That ignorant, ill-spoken oaf!"

"Captain Yaw-Yaw, as you so disparagingly refer to him, is fluent in seven languages and numerous dialects. He is one of my most reliable operatives. He accomplished his mission exactly."

I looked at the beloved faces around me, The Weed's included. My blunder had set all our lives at risk. I bowed my head. "Forgive me. The blame is mine alone."

"Do not reproach yourself, dear Brinnie." My gentle Mary turned consoling eyes upon me. "How could you have known? Did you not mention that *Ariadne* was the only transportation to be had? An ironic coincidence. A dreadful one, but a coincidence nonetheless."

"Do you believe so, Mrs. Garrett?" said Helvitius. "True, the world is full of coincidences. Some can be arranged in advance. I saw to it, at no small expense, that *Ariadne* alone awaited you. Professor Garrett, you were no more than an unwitting pawn in a game beyond your comprehension.

"I was made aware of your itinerary as soon as Mr. Passavant booked your passage. From that moment, the fate of Miss Vesper Holly was in my hands.

"I admit there were trivial errors," Helvitius continued. "Unbeknownst to your worthy Captain Fergus, one of my hirelings signed on as a crew member. His orders were to sink the freighter. He failed to do so. I have made sure he will never fail again."

"We smelt some kind of jiggery-pokery afoot," muttered Slider.

Smiler nodded. "Reeked of skulduggery, it did."

"Murderer a dozen times over!" I exclaimed. "You would have sunk an entire vessel, all hands aboard, to further your evil scheme."

"A necessary sacrifice," Helvitius replied. "No plan is without cost. Incidental expenses, if you will. Whether the crew survived was a matter of complete indifference to me. As for yourselves, I sent *Ariadne* to rescue you."

"The ship I saw!" I cried. "Captain Yaw-Yaw again!"

"Before he could reach you, the freighter was able to proceed on course," Helvitius said. "I had not foreseen Captain Fergus would sail you directly to Hērákleion. But only minor adjustments were required, with the same result. You, Miss Holly, are here in Xanadu at last."

He gestured expansively, as pleased with his surroundings as any suburban Philadelphia homeowner. "Xanadu has been under construction for some years and is yet unfinished. Alas, you will not have the opportunity to inspect all its amenities. But, I assure you, they represent the most advanced technology. The illumination, for example. As you see, I am completely gassified.

"I receive shipments of what raw materials I require; in large part, however, Xanadu is self-sufficient. I have my laboratories and research facilities, an efficient power-generating plant, all the resources I could wish. More than that, Xanadu is my retreat where I set aside my daily cares—a place for quiet meditation, an oasis of relaxation and recreation."

My sweet Mary, charitable toward Helvitius when she believed him dead, abruptly changed her attitude upon seeing him alive. "Oasis? No! A hotbed for your villainy."

"Harsh words, Mrs. Garrett," Helvitius replied, with an amused smile. "Villainy? If you insist on the term, villainy *is* my recreation."

He turned to Dionescu, silent throughout this conversation. I myself had been too shocked at finding Helvitius well and thriving to absorb the full impact of Dionescu's duplicity. Above all, what cut me to the quick was our betrayal by a celebrated author.

"I expected you sooner. It does not please me to be kept waiting." Helvitius spoke in a tone that caused the wretch's mustache to wilt, while his chin sank into his collar. Sweating, Dionescu stammered out the reasons for his delay.

"You should have brought them to me directly," Helvitius said. "You have introduced an element of confusion in an otherwise simple plan." He paused, thoughtful for a moment. "And yet, I admit what you discovered is fascinating. I shall overlook—this time—your failure to carry out my instructions. Yes, I wish to learn more.

"What you shall do," he went on, "is to return to Neopolis and report the tragic, accidental demise of Miss Vesper Holly and party. You shall take over the late Mr. Passavant's research and continue it as your own, as he would have wished you to do—"

"Demise?" Dionescu goggled at him. "Do you imply—? Sir, you did not give me to understand that was your intention."

"Miss Holly has thwarted me too often—not least, in Philadelphia. She has meddled in my business for the last time. What did you expect me to do? As an academic, you can hardly be so naive and innocent."

Dionescu stood up, visibly shaken. "Is this not—extreme?"

"Extremely logical, necessary, and the natural consequences of her past actions. Consider the Moirai, the Three Fates. Clotho, who spins out lives; Lachesis, who measures their duration; and I perform the role of Atropos, who cuts them with her shears, snip-snip-snip.

"You will go to Neopolis tomorrow. Do as I order you. The servants will prepare your usual quarters for the night. Leave us now. Miss Holly and I have, as it were, family matters to conclude."

Dionescu, avoiding our eyes, slunk off like a schoolboy caught cheating on an examination paper.

"Serpent!" I flung at his retreating back. "A viper in our bosom!"

I rounded on Helvitius. "Of all your vile deeds, this ranks

among the most despicable. You, sir, have corrupted one of the world's distinguished scholars."

"Not difficult," said Helvitius. "He was overjoyed at the opportunity. A common human weakness, but human weakness is my source of strength.

"Though an intellectual, he has actually been of use," Helvitius added, "especially in his current archaeological pursuits."

"I didn't think you'd care much about discovering Troy," said Vesper. "There's no money in it. Or do you expect to dig up the city treasury? Don't count on it. The Greeks got there ahead of you."

"Miss Holly, you do me a disservice." Helvitius gave her a wounded look. "I have always taken pleasure in classical antiquity; however, as you point out, there is little material gain in it. But what a dreary world it would be without the joys of art, music, and all such impractical activities. When time permits, I myself have written poetry and found that avocation soothing to the spirit.

"As for treasure in the worldly sense: Among other endeavors, I have turned my attention to a substance offering rewards beyond imagination.

"Unhappily, Miss Holly, you will not be present to admire the full fruition of my labors. But, I can assure you, the object of my research will, in future, be more precious than gold.

"The substance I refer to," Helvitius declared, "is . . . oil."

I knew then that he had gone completely mad.

9

...

"I do not speak of olive oil, castor oil, cod-liver oil, or other such homely, household items," Helvitius said, in answer to Mary's questioning frown. "It is what you Americans quaintly call 'rock oil.' In other words: petroleum.

"My research shows me that petroleum, in all its varied forms, is infinitely versatile. In and of itself, it will be the fuel of the future. Combined with various chemical additives, its usefulness increases a hundredfold. It is priceless, beyond anything the alchemists dreamed of creating. I intend to seek it out—"

"I'm sorry to tell you this," Vesper interrupted. "They've already discovered oil in Pennsylvania. You're just about twenty years too late."

"Furthermore," I put in, "the petroleum of our Common-wealth is the highest quality."

"I am aware of the Titusville fields, and the fellow, Drake— a rank amateur, a retired railroad conductor—who blundered upon them," Helvitius said. "But the oil flow in your native state is a trickle compared with richer deposits elsewhere. My studies convince me that the entire North American continent is pitifully lacking in that product. Where would it be found? In the Texas deserts? The wilds of your Oklahoma Territory? The frozen wastelands of Alaska? Most certainly not in Canada.

"No, Miss Holly, it is here. This corner of the world, I have reason to believe, is floating on tides, seas, oceans of oil. The Bard of Avon speaks of the perfumes of Arabia . . ."

For a moment, I feared The Weed would put in his oar, but he thought better of it and kept silent. Helvitius pressed on:

"The perfumes of Arabia? They waft the scent of petroleum."

"What's that have to do with Troy?" said Vesper. "Do you expect you'll strike oil under King Priam's palace?"

"A ludicrous notion." Helvitius nearly laughed. "No. Vissarlik is devoid of it. As an amusement, it pleases me to finance Dionescu's excavations. I shall permit him to appropriate Mr. Passavant's research as a sop to his vanity. He has, these past several years, published nothing, the equivalent of death in the dark forests of academe. Now not only will he have his Trojan discoveries to write about, Mr. Passavant's work will give him ample material for another treatise as well. He will regain a long-lost reputation."

"I didn't think you cared about anyone's reputation," Vesper said.

"Except for my own, I do not," replied Helvitius. "Dionescu serves me in other ways. As an archaeologist, he can roam from place to place. As a geologist, he can locate petroleum deposits, which he has done admirably. I have secretly purchased enormous tracts of land. My holdings—without boasting, Miss Holly, at the moment I control much of Asia Minor, vast portions of Arabia. If the nations of the world require oil, as they surely will, they must deal with me."

"They won't," Vesper said flatly. "They won't let you get away with it. If they have to, they'll invade and take the whole business from you. Wars have been fought for less."

"Not in this case," replied Helvitius. "Powerful private interests throughout Europe stand to profit along with me. For the rest, the Ottoman Empire is falling to pieces. Who is best able to snatch them up? I am. My seat of government will be here in Xanadu, not Istanbul."

My head spun at the monster's overweening ambition. He actually believed he could make himself Sultan of Arabia. A madman's dream. Listening to him, however, I wondered if he might be dangerously sane.

Vesper, as always, introduced a note of common sense. "That depends on who wins the war."

"To me, it makes no difference," said Helvitius. "I enjoy the most amicable relationship with the Sultan; and, likewise, with the Czar. In this squabble between them, the only winner will be: myself. I will set the terms of any treaty, they will agree to them. They must. And so must all the rest of the world."

Vesper remarked that he expected a great deal from his oil holdings.

"That is the least of it," he said. "There is one decisive factor. It has emerged from my research. I have been able to take certain petroleum derivatives and combine them with various additives. Nitrogen, hydrogen . . . "

I was sorry Vesper had opened the question, for Helvitius began prosing about distillation, titration, fractionation, catalysis until my eyelids drooped.

But as he droned on about the properties of methyl benzene, carbon, oxygen, and so on, Vesper sat upright and rigid. The more she listened to him, the paler grew her face.

Helvitius smiled in satisfaction. "You have an excellent grasp of organic chemistry, Miss Holly. You will understand the implications of my discovery."

Vesper nodded slowly. "You can blow things up."

Helvitius clapped his hands. "Brava! Precisely! But that is to put it mildly. Call it an explosive compound more powerful than the world has ever known. In comparison, dynamite is a penny firecracker.

"Its destructive force is a joy to behold, most exhilarating," he went on. "The product, at the moment, is highly combustible, but unstable, difficult to control. That problem will be easily solved.

"Since I am its inventor"—Helvitius steepled his fingers—"with all due modesty, I have named it 'Helvolene.'

"But enough shop talk. I have personal matters to take up. You have been a worthy opponent, Miss Holly. I see no reason why, at the end, we should not be civil to each other."

"I do," said Vesper.

Helvitius sighed. "I feared that might be your attitude. Miss Holly, you are intelligent enough to realize, and to face the fact: I have won and you have lost."

Vesper said nothing. The dear girl does not enjoy losing, which is why she seldom does.

"Now, alas," Helvitius said, "we come to the moment of Atropos."

"I knew you'd get around to that," replied Vesper.

"Do not be overly dismayed," Helvitius said. "It is a fate every mortal shares. You will, I know, accept yours with grace and dignity.

"I have become more philosophical about the subject," he continued. "Mellower, more kindly disposed, if you will. Not one of us is given to know beforehand the hour of our departure. Which is, no doubt, a blessing.

"I apply the same principle to you. Miss Holly, you will surely die. That much is certain. But when? Today? Tomorrow? Next week? Next year? And how? Where? In the world at large, these are impenetrable mysteries. Here in Xanadu, it is I who make those determinations.

"Now, Miss Holly, shall we dine?"

EXCEPT for a faculty banquet at our University of Pennsylvania, where I had the impression the boiled fish was looking at me, our dinner with Helvitius was the most bizarre in my experience. Vesper and I had, on occasion, shared a repast with him—also in unhappy conditions. But this was grotesque, nightmarish beyond expression.

He had, as a kind of appetizer, boasted of his scheme to acquire every drop of oil throughout the Arabian peninsula. He had revealed his invention of the diabolical Helvolene, which presumably could blow up large segments of the world. He aspired to become a sultan. He had confessed to corrupting a distinguished scholar. He had pronounced our death sentence. Worse, he had subjected us to the cruelest of torments: the agony of suspense. It would have been kinder to dispatch us out of hand and be done with it.

And yet—I can hardly bring myself to admit it—the weirdest aspect of this event was: We had a very good time.

The atmosphere was cordial, collegial—apart from a few heated exchanges, which can occur in the course of any dinner party.

Had we become resigned to our fate? Had we so abandoned hope that nothing held significance for us? Had the certainty of death liberated us from all trivial considerations? No. I was sure that Vesper, and each one of us, continued to ponder the best means of escape. But that, for the time being, was relegated to the back of our minds.

Perhaps it was the food, as excellent as any served at Philadelphia's luxurious La Pierre House.

I had expected to dine in the traditional manner of this part of the world, seated on our cushions and communally sharing dishes. On the contrary. Helvitius clapped his hands; servants arrived instantly and, like a conjuring trick, set up chairs and a festive table gleaming with sterling silverware and Baccarat crystal goblets. I would not have been surprised to see Helvitius change into formal dinner attire. He only removed his turban and undid his sash to give himself more freedom of movement while he personally served our food.

"I trust you will find this acceptable." He gestured at an array of silver buckets holding chilled bottles of champagne. "Dom Pérignon '68. Miss Holly, may I have the honor of filling your glass?"

"Touch it not!" I cried to her, springing from my chair. "Like the cocoa he offered us in El Dorado, it is poison!"

"My dear Professor Garrett," said Helvitius, popping the cork, "while '68 may not be the greatest of all vintage years—for which I apologize—in no way can Dom Pérignon be called poison. Do you believe me so crude as to commit such an outrage against good taste? Cocoa is one thing, Dom Pérignon is another."

"He has a point, Brinnie," Vesper said.

"I swear to you," declared Helvitius, "this divine beverage is uncontaminated."

To prove his claim, he downed some good swallows and served the rest to us. Did we trust him? Surely not. But, as I said, it had no great importance one way or another. In any case, I detected nothing lethal.

From then on, it was one course after the other, punctuated by long-stemmed cups of sherbet garnished with rose petals to cleanse our palates and increase our enjoyment of the dishes that followed.

Apart from The Weed, I have never seen anyone attack food with more intensity than Helvitius. He chomped away with his powerful, carnivorous teeth; his face had taken on a rosy glow. His shock of white hair and his fleshy cheeks made him look like a very large and evil cherub.

He was, throughout our dinner, at his most expansive—a perfect host and model of courtesy. At the end, after passing around trays of figs, dates, and pistachio nuts, he leaned back and glanced affably around the table.

"You no doubt have wondered why I chose to name my retreat Xanadu."

I did not recall anyone raising that subject. He continued nonetheless:

"First, it is to honor and express my deepest admiration for Kubla Khan."

"I would have thought," said Vesper, "you'd have more for

his grandfather. Genghis Khan had the notion of conquering the whole world. The two of you have something in common."

"Indeed, we do," said Helvitius. "The estimable Genghis raised brutality to a fine art. I respect and revere him for that. But my allusion, as you surely recognize, is to that poetic masterpiece by Mr. Samuel Taylor Coleridge: 'Kubla Khan.'"

The Weed had been too occupied with his dinner to be intrusive. Now, having polished off the remaining pistachio nuts, he flung himself into the conversation.

Of all times and places for him to start spouting! But there was no stopping him. I could only roll my eyes as he began:

> *"In Xanadu did Kubla Khan*
> *A stately pleasure-dome decree:*
> *Where Alph, the sacred river, ran*
> *Through caverns measureless to man*
> *Down to a sunless sea."*

"And then something about 'ground.'" The Weed turned to Vesper. "You know it, Carrots. How does it go?"

Before Vesper could answer, Helvitius lifted a finger and continued the passage:

> *"So twice five miles of fertile ground*
> *With walls and towers were girdled round:*
> *And there were gardens bright with sinuous rills . . . "*

From then on, while Smiler and Slider listened eagerly and Mary toyed with the silverware, they racketed lines back and forth as if it were a three-way match in that newest fad, lawn tennis.

"There are moments that reach the sublime," said Helvitius, pausing a moment to sip his champagne. "'A savage place'—ah, yes." He raised his goblet to Vesper:

> *"A savage place! as holy and enchanted*
> *As e'er beneath a waning moon was haunted*
> *By woman wailing for her demon-lover!"*

I saw The Weed bristle, half rising, and feared I might have to sit on him. Vesper ignored the pointed glance from Helvitius, and what could have turned into an awkward incident went by.

"Remarkable," said Helvitius, unperturbed, "how Coleridge speaks to our present conditions. Here, for example:

> *"And 'mid this tumult Kubla heard from far*
> *Ancestral voices prophesying war!"*

"And," he added, "still more appropriate to our little soirée:

> *"A damsel with a dulcimer*
> *In a vision once I saw . . ."*

"Although I cannot provide a banjo, on which I understand you perform charmingly," he said to Vesper, "I believe a dulcimer could be located. If you would favor us with a musical moment—"

"I'm not in the mood," replied Vesper.

"Alas." Helvitius sighed. "As Coleridge expresses it so perfectly:

> "Could I revive within me
> Her symphony and song,
> To such a deep delight 'twould win me,
> That with music loud and long,
> I would build that dome in air,
> That sunny dome! those caves of ice!
> And all who heard should see them there,
> And all should cry, Beware! Beware!"

"For there is another aspect to Xanadu—my own Xanadu—I have not yet mentioned," said Helvitius, interrupting his recitation. "'I would build that dome . . .' Yes, it is my intention, as far as it lies within my modest powers, to build my Xanadu according to the details mentioned in the poem.

"Has ever an architect designed an edifice to match one described in a work of literature? Unique in the history of the world. Here the magical phrases of Coleridge will take on solid existence.

"Xanadu is not yet complete," Helvitius continued. "I have labored off and on for some years, but it remains unfinished."

The Weed glanced at me. I expected him to make some comparison with my Etruscan history. Helvitius gave him no chance to speak.

"Unfinished," he repeated. "Like the poem itself. As you surely know, 'Kubla Khan' is only the fragment of a masterpiece. It was abandoned on the verge of the poet's greatest triumph. Destroyed, shattered!"

"By a real-estate fellow, isn't that right, sir?" The Weed said to me. "Coleridge was writing away, fired up with inspiration, when along comes a chap from a nearby village— Porlock, wasn't it?

"Some silly matter of business. Rent, leases," The Weed pressed on. "He wouldn't go away. He made such a nuisance of himself, Coleridge had to leave off his work and come out of his study to deal with him."

"Exactly so, Mr. Passavant," said Helvitius. "When Coleridge at last returned to his desk, his inspiration had fled, vanished. He could never recapture it. His poem remained forever incomplete, ruined by a barbaric real-estate agent. What a crime against literature!"

I had nothing but sympathy for poor Coleridge confronted with an intrusive visitor. Helvitius pursued his subject.

"Not only shall I finish building Xanadu," he declared, "but when I have a few idle hours, I shall conclude what Coleridge began."

I could not allow this to pass unchallenged.

"How dare you?" I burst out. "Tamper with a work of poetic genius? That is more despicable than your fiendish Helvolene!"

I shook my finger with extreme disapproval. "What then? Will you next glue arms on the Venus de Milo? Affix a head on the Victory of Samothrace? Insensitivity worthy of your idol, Genghis Khan. No! Of Attila the Hun!"

It surprised me that neither Vesper nor The Weed joined in my outrage. Mary and the twins were likewise silent, seeming to drowse. I could, in fact, barely keep my own eyes open.

I feared that Shiva's Revenge had attacked again. Numbness spread upward from my toes. Then the horrible truth dawned upon me.

"Liar! Perjurer!" My words came out slurred, my tongue felt too big for my mouth. "You swore to us! Scoundrel! Poisoner! The champagne—"

"I spoke the absolute truth." The vile creature dabbed his lips with a monogrammed napkin. Before my eyes, the initial *H* grew larger and larger until it entangled me. The last thing I heard was the voice of Helvitius:

"No, Professor Garrett, it was not the Dom Pérignon. It was the pistachio nuts."

11

...

IT took a few moments to convince myself I was still alive, and a few additional moments to realize our dinner party with Helvitius had not been a figment of my imagination. It was not a nightmare. The nightmare was only beginning. I cried out in horror at what I saw.

On the tiled floor of a spacious but unfurnished chamber lay the outstretched forms of my loved ones. I staggered to them, with terror, grief, and rage I cannot describe. It flashed through my mind: Had the *chiron*'s medication given me a protective immunity, sparing me from the full effect of the poisoned pistachio nuts while those nearest and dearest had succumbed?

But then—the flood of joyous relief was as great as my despair—Vesper and Mary, lying side by side, stirred from what I now understood to be a heavily drugged sleep. Smiler and Slider blinked open their eyes at the same time. Only The Weed, who had stuffed himself with more of those traitorous pistachios than the rest of us, continued snoring.

Seeing my dear ones alive, unharmed, and well on the way to recovery, I turned my attention to our place of confinement.

The iron-bound door, as I determined, was tightly shut, locked from outside. I realized we were in a sort of vestibule, for I glimpsed other chambers connecting with it. Smiler and Slider were fully awake and on their feet. I beckoned for them to come with me, hoping to find some possible means of escape.

We entered a suite of apartments with latticed dividers and wrought-iron grilles at the windows. Lightly furnished with divans, cushions, and silk draperies, the establishment appeared ready and waiting for occupancy.

If Helvitius was gassified, he also had water laid on. In the center of this honeycomb of chambers, under a domed ceiling, a fountain bubbled in a little atrium or inner courtyard. For a prison, it was not unattractive; I was grateful Helvitius had not chosen to fling us into a foul dungeon. Until I understood what I was seeing.

Leaving the twins to continue exploring, I hurried back to Mary and Vesper. The Weed, yawning, was inquiring about breakfast. When I reported where we were, Mary gasped.

"Are you telling us, Brinnie," she exclaimed, "that we are prisoners in—in a harem?"

"But, at least, with excellent facilities." I added that Helvitius had obviously planned these accommodations for a future Madame Helvitius—or, as accepted in these parts, perhaps a couple of them.

I stopped short, aghast at the implications of my words. Mary stiffened in shock:

"Does that monster intend—? Are we to be at his disposal? This goes beyond all bounds of propriety—"

"Dearest angel, it will not happen," I declared. "Never! I will defend your honor with my life."

"Brinnie," answered Mary, "do you forget I am a daughter of Philadelphia? I am perfectly capable of defending my honor myself, and so is our dear Vesper."

Of that, I replied, I had every confidence. Moreover, since Helvitius had installed us in relative comfort, he surely meant to keep us alive for some while.

"No," said Vesper. "Do the arithmetic, Brinnie. These are women's quarters. He holds Mary and me here; the four of you could be . . . subtracted. At any moment."

"Carrots is right," put in The Weed. "We can't guess how long he'll play his game. An hour? Days? Five minutes?"

"If we don't know how much time we have," said Vesper, "we'd better assume we have none at all. Which means: We start doing something now."

Smiler and Slider, meanwhile, had come back from their tour of inspection.

"That Helvitius fellow's got quite a factory out there," Smiler said.

"We saw some of it from a back window," said Slider. "Chimneys smoking away. What looks like a nice little power plant. A pumping station. Even a rail spur."

"I'll want to see that," Vesper said. "It fits in with something I have in mind. Last night, Helvitius may have told us more than he meant to do."

"More?" said Mary. "I thought he told us everything. The creature never stopped talking."

"It's the poem," Vesper said. "If he's building Xanadu to match the one in 'Kubla Khan,' do the lines give us any clue? A way out of here?"

It is always a joy to see Vesper's powerful intellect at work. This time, I feared she might be on the wrong track. Reflecting on the passages in Coleridge, I found nothing of help. A pleasure dome? Yes, very well, there was in fact a dome. Walls and towers? Gardens? I granted all that.

But the rest, as I pointed out, made no sense. Alph, the sacred river? Caverns measureless to man? A sunless sea? I doubted that Helvitius could produce such things.

"That's true, Brinnie," replied Vesper. "I don't understand how it fits in—if it fits in at all. Helvitius can't copy every detail. He probably had to skip a lot of it and settle for something just to remind him of Xanadu.

"What sticks in my mind . . ." she went on. "All right, Brinnie, answer me this. Did you notice anything about the sherbet?"

I admitted I did not, other than it was pleasantly refreshing.

"Refreshingly cool?" Vesper said. "And the champagne? Nicely chilled?" she pressed on as I shook my head, still puzzled. "In silver buckets—of what?"

"Ice, naturally," I said.

"Then," said Vesper, "where did he keep it? What about:

> *I would build that dome in air,*
> *That sunny dome! those caves of ice!"*

"The old Persian kings had blocks of ice hauled down from the mountains," said The Weed, "and stored them in the palace cellars."

"Tobias, old Persian kings are no help," I told him. "We

are in extremis. Every moment counts. We can speculate and try to solve these riddles while time runs out. We must undertake prompt action."

As Vesper had been citing Coleridge, a vigorous plan had formed in my mind. Unless Helvitius intended killing us by slow starvation, I had to assume we would be fed. He, or his hirelings, must sooner or later open the door to bring in our rations.

"Let us be ready for that moment," I urged. "We shall set upon them, take them by surprise, burst free—"

"Not free," Vesper said. "We'd still be in Xanadu."

"Better out and on the loose than sitting locked in a room. It's a fighting chance." The Weed had a glint in his eye; I had seen it before. It usually signified he was on the verge of doing something stupid. But this time, I was glad for his support.

Vesper and Mary, to my disappointment, showed a lack of enthusiasm. Nevertheless, I enlarged on my order of battle. Taking a firm tone of command, I explained that I would stand at the doorway, ready to spring, with Smiler and Slider on my left and right. Vesper and Mary would be protected in our midst, The Weed behind them as rear guard.

"Although we have no weapons," I told them, "our best resource is courage and determination—"

"I cannot entirely approve of such violent behavior. . . ." Mary hesitated. "But—but I have a weapon. Brinnie, I am armed."

"Bless you!" I cried as Mary drew a piece of silverware from her sleeve and pressed it in my hand.

"I was not brought up to steal people's table settings,"

Mary said, "but in this case, I had no compunction. This was all I dared to take, hoping one small item would not be missed."

"Sweet angel," I replied, "it will serve the purpose."

"Brinnie, you're my fierce tiger," Vesper said. "But—that's a butter knife."

Ah yes, well, so it was. I reminded Vesper that her father and I had spent some days at the Shaolin Temple, where the famous warrior monks demonstrated that even chopsticks can become lethal implements.

We waited then, silent, strengthening our resolve, The Weed fidgeting impatiently. I began wondering if Helvitius had chosen to inflict slow starvation on us.

After a time, I heard approaching footfalls. I ordered all to take their positions. The chilling thought came to me: Was it breakfast—or the moment of Atropos?

Bolts rasped as they were drawn back. I took a firm grip on the butter knife. The door flung open. I leaped forward.

Or so I would have done. That instant, a cannonball struck me in the pit of my stomach.

12

...

THE sudden impact sent me reeling, stumbling against Slider on the one hand, Smiler on the other. The crucial moment of attack had passed; the door slammed shut and bolted once again. I sprawled to the tiles, flat on my back, grappling with flailing arms and legs.

It was not a cannonball that felled me, but the bulletlike head of Professor-Doctor Mirko Dionescu.

The scholar must have had a skull of solid bone, for it completely knocked the wind out of me. The twins pulled him off and set him on his feet. Vesper and Mary helped me up. I clutched my solar plexus and struggled to catch my breath.

"Treacherous academic!" I shouted between gasps. "No better than your vile master!"

I had dropped the butter knife, which I gladly would have used. Instead, I threw myself at him, ready to throttle him with my bare hands.

"Stop, dear Brinnie!" Mary cried. "For mercy's sake! The man is wounded."

True, he did not look well. But my blood was up. Had Mary not held me back, I would not have been accountable for my actions.

Keeping her own temper in check, Vesper demanded to know what business he had with us.

"Yes, wretched little man!" I picked up the butter knife and brandished it under his nose. "How dare you show your face in our presence? I should carve your mustache to the roots!"

"I am here to share your fate," Dionescu replied. "I, too, am a prisoner.

"I came to save you," he hurried on. "Miss Holly, I swear to you by the last shreds of academic integrity that remain to me—"

"Shreds?" I cried. "You have not so much as a fig leaf of human decency. Sir, you disgrace your profession."

"Hear him out anyway," Vesper said.

I folded my arms and turned a skeptical glance on Dionescu. He averted his eyes and sniffled pathetically.

"I never imagined," he continued, "that Helvitius, monster though he is, had designs on your life. He led me to believe he wished to discuss urgent business matters, not your extermination. Alone in my sleeping quarters, I suffered such torments of guilt and pangs of conscience that I could no longer bear them, tortures far worse than anything Helvitius could devise.

"As a frequent visitor to Xanadu, I knew its various chambers and corridors, and I found my way to your place of imprisonment. The guard at the door recognized me as a familiar figure and was glad when I offered to relieve him for a short while. I intended, during his absence, to set you free and guide you from the building."

"I don't think Helvitius would have been pleased with you," Vesper said.

Dionescu nodded. "I realized my actions would make him an implacable enemy and put my life at risk. I was willing to make that sacrifice. Aiding in your escape, I, likewise, might escape from his power over me.

"But this was not to be." Dionescu sighed. "My behavior aroused the guard's suspicions. Within moments, even as I struggled to unbolt the door, he came back with his comrades. They seized me, frog-marched me to Helvitius in his private chambers, and reported what I had attempted to do.

"He did not rage at me," Dionescu said. "It would have been more human had he done so. But no, his wrath was icy, frigid as his evil heart. He had a sneer of contempt and mockery on his lips—and then he struck me. Not in the heat of anger, but deliberately, with calculation, in cold blood. Yes! He assaulted me! With a violence I thought existed only in the realms of higher education.

"I pleaded for your lives. And, I confess, for my own as well. I reminded him of the invaluable services I had performed, the pinpointing of oil deposits that set the seal of his power in Baku, Ploiesti, the hinterlands of Arabia. I vowed to be still more diligent on his behalf.

"He laughed at me. 'Professor-Doctor, are you so prideful

as to believe I cannot replace you with a snap of my fingers? I can cite a crowded roster of distinguished individuals who thirst for such an opportunity.'

"He looked down at me as if I were an ant to be flattened under his thumb. 'Since you are so concerned for the lives of Miss Vesper Holly and her party, you shall join them. Their fate shall be yours. A scholar with a conscience is too dangerous to exist.'"

Dionescu hung his head. I have never seen an academic so downcast and woebegone. He clasped his hands in a prayerful gesture: "I do not deserve your forgiveness; I beg it, nevertheless."

"Traitor!" I exclaimed. "You have cost our lives—"

"Brinnie, please remember we are Philadelphians," Mary said. "It is our sacred duty to forgive our enemies. Besides, it will make him feel better."

I replied that I had no doubt it would, but forgiveness did nothing to save us from the fatal predicament he had put us in.

"What I want to know," Vesper said to him, "is why you got tangled up with Helvitius in the first place. You told us you wanted to get free of his power over you. A scholar of your distinction? What power could he have?"

"Alas, Miss Holly, my story is not unique. With variations in details, it has led to the downfall of countless colleagues. As I now look back on it, I am certain Helvitius was behind the situation from the very first. His hand forged the links in the shameful chain of events. At the time, I did not realize it. Despite my years at the University of Cludj, I still retained a measure of innocence.

"As I indicated to you when we first met, I had published nothing since my *Short Dictionary of Classical Antiquities*. A deplorable hiatus, and a dangerous one. I had become too absorbed—shall I say obsessed?—with Troy, the great city of Homer and of history. I devoted every ounce of energy to reading and research, at the expense of my seminar and lecturing duties. I grew unwilling to serve on committees. I attended few faculty meetings; eventually, none at all. I was, in consequence, an academic leper.

"The Regents of Cludj refused funding for my proposed archaeological expedition, though I assured them I knew precisely the location of ancient Ilium. My exhaustive research convinced me it was at Vissarlik. If I could uncover it, the resulting textbooks and illustrated popular volumes would be my life preserver, masterwork, and crowning glory of my career.

"I spare you an account of the machinations and schemes of my rival professors, the malice, the savagery of their attacks upon me. In the end, my enemies triumphed. I was summarily dismissed from my position.

"I was forced to make my way in a world as cold, heartless, and brutal as any institution of higher learning. I had spent my savings on my investigations; barely a penny remained. What was an unemployed intellectual to do?

"I sold my household goods and clothing and moved to a cramped attic in the reeking slums of Bucharest. To keep body and soul together—what little remained of either—I became a literary critic for the public press."

Though furious at him, I could not hear his confession unmoved.

"Poor chap," I said. "Poor chap."

"At that moment of my deepest despair," Dionescu continued, "I received an invitation to dine in a private room at the finest hotel in Bucharest. Naturally, I accepted. My host, as it turned out—"

"Dr. Desmond Helvitius," Vesper said.

Dionescu nodded. "Thus began my entrapment. He knew all that had befallen me. He promised unlimited funds for my expedition. In exchange, I would locate petroleum deposits and act as a false front for his acquisition of properties. A devil's bargain.

"There is one thing more I have not mentioned. In the course of my excavations, I discovered indisputable evidence that so shocked me . . ."

13

...

DIONESCU had to take a couple of breaths before going on. "I have been digging in the wrong place. Vissarlik is not the site of Troy.

"Possibly I misinterpreted some aspects of my research. Perhaps the sources I relied on were flawed. Perhaps I miscalculated. Or, in my obsession, I deluded myself. I wanted the ruins to be those of Troy and let myself believe they were. Pretended they were. Pretense is no longer possible. Every scrap of evidence I have unearthed contradicts me."

"But you did find something," Vesper said.

"A trading outpost," Dionescu replied. "Authentically ancient, yes. The Trojans built and settled it. As far as I can determine, they named it Neopolis—"

"Like the village?" put in Vesper.

Dionescu nodded. "There is no question in my mind. The inhabitants there are truly descendants of Trojan refugees. The Greeks destroyed the outpost in the course of the war, burned it to the ground as ruthlessly as they did Troy itself. Given time, Neopolis might have grown and prospered, but it was not the great city I dreamed of finding."

"And the real Troy?" said Vesper.

"At Hissarlik. Schliemann has discovered the true site. Upstart, amateur he may be—but he is right. I am wrong."

Such an admission took me aback and startled Vesper herself. Dionescu went on:

"Until now, I have told only one person: Helvitius. Two weeks ago, I informed him, in all conscience, I could no longer persist in what I knew to be a sham and a fraud. I was in despair over my mistake; and, as well, my entanglement with him had become abhorrent. I wished no further connection between us.

"He shrugged away my declaration. 'You tell me you have not discovered Troy? Do not be concerned. One ancient ruin is like another. Who is to say which is which? A matter of opinion. Who shall agree when doctors disagree?

"'I shall bring all my considerable influence to bear on your colleagues and the public alike, convincing them that your findings are correct and Schliemann is a fraud—easily done, for he has no qualifications or credentials. I have the means to turn him into a laughingstock and yourself into the most brilliant archaeologist of our day, your place in history secured.'

"The enormity—yes, the obscenity—of his proposal left me speechless," Dionescu said. "Then Helvitius added, 'Your resignation is a minor inconvenience, but I shall accept it.' He smiled—oh, those terrifying teeth of his! 'Answer me one question: How long will I permit you to live after that? You know too much of my dealings. Your span of existence? Let me put it thus: Do not buy yourself a winter overcoat.'

"I had not the courage to defy him and agreed to perpetuate the fraud," Dionescu admitted. "Now it makes no difference. Let him do his worst. I am a prisoner under a death sentence, but free to be an honest man."

Dionescu, exhausted by his injuries and his shameful account, turned from us and slumped down in a corner of the chamber.

"Do you believe any of that?" I murmured to Vesper. "He lied when he told us he found Troy. Is he lying now when he says he did not? It would not surprise me if he had some deceitful scheme in mind."

"I don't know," said Vesper. "He looks miserable enough to be telling the truth."

"What if he is still a creature of Helvitius?" I insisted. "Sent here to spy upon us?"

"Whatever he is or isn't, let him alone for now," Vesper said. "I want to think about ice. Caves of ice. Does Helvitius have something like them?"

Vesper pointed beyond the latticed window. "The sun's up. It has to be blazing hot out there. But, in here, it's very comfortable."

"Well, now, Miss Vesper, funny you mention it," said Slider, "but when Smiler and I were poking around back there, it was pretty cool, too. I believe I remarked on it at the time."

"So you did," Smiler agreed. "And I even said to you those

harem ladies could be chilly, parading around in their next-to-nothings."

"As we've heard tell that's what they do," added Slider.

"Cold air. Caves of ice," Vesper said. "They fit together."

"Well done, Carrots!" The Weed clapped his hands. "Deciphering a poem—that's as much fun as deciphering inscriptions."

"Tobias, fun does not enter into it." I was about to suggest he would do well to take the possibility of death from one moment to the next with a little more gravity. But then Smiler broke in:

"Slider and I saw some openings in the walls. There's one in every room."

"The biggest in that fountain courtyard," Slider said.

"I'll have a look," said Vesper. "Could they be vents of some kind?"

"Like the flue in a fireplace chimney?" said Mary. "Air comes out. Brinnie, you know how you hate those drafts."

"No." Vesper's face fell. "That won't work."

"Dear girl, why ever not?" I said. "It makes excellent sense."

"Law of physics." Vesper shook her head. "Hot air rises. Cold air sinks. I thought I'd figured it out. I'll have to go at it some other way."

"Miss Holly, if you would allow me . . ." Dionescu must have been eavesdropping on our conversation. I had no idea how long he had been standing behind us.

"I could not help overhearing. Your analysis is correct. Helvitius allowed me to observe the inner workings of Xanadu. He boasted that he had a constant supply of ice carted down from the high mountains and stored in the building's substructure. I am unfamiliar with the poem you refer to. However, the phrase 'caves of ice' would certainly be applicable."

"Right," said Vesper, "but that's not all the answer. How does the air circulate upward?"

"An arrangement of fans operated by belts and pulleys," Dionescu said. "Cold air is driven through a honeycomb of vents that serve the upper chambers. I give that monster credit, he is an excellent engineer. The system is remarkably effective."

"Twins," said Vesper, "let's go see those rooms."

As Smiler and Slider had reported, the largest of the vents was in the courtyard, across from the small fountain. A lattice of wrought-iron curlicues and arabesques, set into the masonry of the wall, blocked all but the stream of cool air. Vesper knelt and peered through the openings. Dionescu fished a box of matches from his pocket, struck a light, and held it close to the lattice. The draft blew it out immediately.

"I can't see beyond a foot or so," Vesper said. "It looks like a chute. It's big enough—we could slide or squeeze our way—if it goes straight down. What if it doesn't? Are there any turns or angles? Does it stay the same diameter or does it get narrower? If we try to go through, we don't want to get stuck like a cork in a bottleneck."

She addressed these comments to Dionescu, who regretfully shook his head. "I am ignorant of the structural details. In any case, the passage is barred."

"Temporarily." Vesper glanced at Smiler and Slider.

The twins needed no further instruction. The spaces between the curlicues gave them room enough to get a strong grip. They heaved and wrestled, hardly stopping to catch their breath. The lattice stubbornly resisted their attack. Smiler and Slider gritted their teeth, bent all their efforts, and, at last, the whole iron frame tore loose in a shower of broken masonry.

Vesper sprang to the jagged opening and cupped a hand to her ear. She tossed a good-sized chunk of masonry into the vent and listened again.

"I can't hear it hit bottom," she said. "What that means, I don't know. But we'll find out."

"Dear girl," I protested, "are you suggesting we go plunging into unknown depths?"

"Of course not," Vesper said.

I heaved a sigh of relief.

"Not right this minute," she added.

Helvitius did not come to see us during the course of that day. I expected him to gloat and further torment us by reminding us of the moment of Atropos, as it pleased him to call it. But he did not. I could not decide which was worse: his presence or his absence, his cruel mockery or inscrutable silence.

More to the point, he did not feed us. We received neither breakfast nor lunch. This, perhaps, was just as well. We could work without interruption, for Vesper kept us extremely busy.

First, following her instructions, we pulled down all the

silken swags and draperies from the walls and tore them into narrow strips. Next, we triple-braided them into a single long cord. With the help of Smiler and Slider, Vesper knotted together a sling, or bosun's chair, that could lower us, one by one, into the vent.

Dionescu, all thumbs when it came to manual dexterity, was pathetically eager to give us added information. He described, as best he recalled, a drainage conduit that carried away water from the melting ice into a shallow pool, a catchment basin outside the walls.

"That could be Alph," Vesper said. "And the sunless sea."

I was too tired and hungry to analyze any more Coleridge. Also, I had graver concerns. As we rested a few moments, I drew Vesper aside and shared my thoughts with her.

I frankly admitted my doubts regarding Dionescu. Whether or not he was a spy for Helvitius, his ambition to discover Troy had been shattered. Would it not suit his interest, then, if he alone escaped? He could, as Helvitius suggested, claim The Weed's research for himself.

"As for Helvitius," I said, "is it possible that we are doing exactly what he expects? Has he foreseen our every move? Does he mean to let us believe we have found a way to freedom; then, at the end, snatch hope away from us? What worse torture?"

"Could be," Vesper said. "But if we don't take the chance, we're lost. There's no way to guess what Helvitius has in mind. All we know is what *we* have in mind."

Then arose yet another torment. We had not eaten all day. Late in the afternoon, when our appetites were at their sharpest, the guards hastily shoved in a large communal pot. Vesper warned us not to touch it.

"Drugged again? Poisoned? Or not? Let it be. That's one risk we don't need to take."

So, with our stomachs growling in protest, we tried to doze and husband our strength. We had agreed, meantime, that our only course, assuming we got free of Xanadu, was to strike across country and make our way back to Neopolis. Safely there, we would contemplate our next step.

Just after sundown, we set our plan in motion. The twins had anchored one end of the rope around the fountain's iron ornaments. Dionescu had volunteered to go first. With Vesper's approval, we hitched him up and lowered him into the vent.

The darkness swallowed him. Smiler and Slider paid out the line; the rest of us took up the slack. As agreed, one tug signaled danger and we would immediately haul him back.

It was then my doubts assailed me. Were there hazards we could not foresee? What if Dionescu got himself stuck? If he did reach the ice cave, would he betray us again? And, most chilling, was Helvitius waiting at the bottom?

After what felt like an eternity, the rope twitched. Once.

I held my breath. A second tug followed, then a third. We pulled up the empty bosun's chair. Smiler climbed into it and we lowered him away. Three tugs gave us hope that he was safe.

Mary went next. I embraced my gentle angel—and told her a lie. I promised all would be well.

"Brinnie," she replied, "I do not expect it to be otherwise."

Slider followed. With fewer of us aboveground to take the strain on the rope, our efforts had grown more difficult; but the continuing signals of safe passage encouraged us.

"Dear girl," I said, as Vesper prepared for her turn, "should aught go amiss, if we are doomed to fail, one day we all shall meet in a brighter, happier place."

"Philadelphia?" she said.

14

. . .

THEN she was gone. The Weed and I lowered away as rapidly as we dared. Her three tugs on the line should have reassured me, but I could not blot out my fear that Helvitius and his ruffians lay in ambush to seize us one after the other.

"Here you go, sir," said The Weed as we hauled up the sling.

He gave me a big, happy grin. He had that glint in his eye—he actually seemed to enjoy risking his neck. And mine.

"I'll be right with you, sir," he said, as if that was meant to cheer me.

Vesper and I have been in more than our share of cells and crypts. Though I never mentioned it to her, I do not feel at ease in confined spaces. Even the stacks of the Library Company in Philadelphia induce sweaty palms. The air vent in Xanadu was the closest thing to a straitjacket.

It was, as best I could determine, lined with coarse plaster, not designed to withstand plummeting bodies. Parts of the surface were already cracking and crumbling. Above, The Weed paid out the rope as fast as he could. I landed heavily, shuddering in the chilly air: the "caves of ice," as Dionescu had suggested.

A shape loomed in front of me. Helvitius had trapped us, exactly as I feared. With a furious cry, I threw up my arms, ready to grapple with my attacker.

"Hush, Brinnie. Don't make such a racket," warned Vesper. "The drainage ditch—Alph, the sacred river—it's just ahead. We're waiting for you."

"Go with them," I said. "Tobias and I shall follow you momentarily."

She vanished into the darkness. I had barely untangled myself from the ropes when an avalanche of loose gravel and broken plaster poured down the vent. It was all I could do to jump aside and escape being buried.

"Is that you, sir?" The Weed's voice was muffled by the wall of debris.

"What, for heaven's sake, have you done?" I had expected The Weed, as the last one remaining in the harem, to have simply slid down the rope. I tried to clear away the rubble choking the vent. Instead of finding a pair of feet, I groped at The Weed's head and mop of hair clotted with plaster and pebbles. "Why are you upside down?"

"The walls were caving in. Couldn't wait, you see, or I'd have been blocked off. Just had to dive right in headfirst so I'd have my hands free to dig my way through."

"Well, then, get about doing it," I told him. "Hurry. Come out of there."

"Sorry, sir. Afraid I'm stuck."

"You're what?" I admit I was losing patience with him. Meantime, I had been scrabbling at the heap of gravel. The Weed stayed where he was.

"Stuck, sir. I think my legs are caught."

"Shake them free!" I cried. "Don't dawdle. Everyone's gone on ahead."

"Can't seem to do it. You run along with them, sir. Never mind about me. I'll manage somehow. If I don't—well, you just tell Carrots my last thoughts were of her."

"Stop that nonsense!" I was practically shouting at him. "Or your last thoughts will be of me dragging you out by the ears."

I was sorry now that I had been vexed with him. The Weed's predicament was more serious than I had supposed. I clawed at the gravel until my hands were bloody. The Weed did the best he could, but he was too cramped to be much use. I would have been glad for a shovel, even a garden trowel. Then it dawned on me. I had an implement: the butter knife my dear Mary had stolen.

At some point, unthinking, I had slipped it into my pocket and forgotten about it. I snatched it out and doubled my efforts, chipping and hacking at the mouth of the vent. I nearly despaired when the blunt end snapped off; but this, in fact, turned out to be an advantage, for now I had a sharper tool.

I cleared away enough rubble for The Weed to thrust out a hand, then both arms. I took a good grip on them and pulled steadily while he pushed with his feet. Suddenly he came loose, which sent me staggering back. He crawled out, shook himself, and stamped around, rubbing his limbs.

"Why, sir," he blurted, "you saved my life."

"Tobias, please, no melodramatics." I urged him to stop bouncing and get a move on.

"But you did," The Weed insisted. "You really did. Very decent of you, sir."

I tried to fend off his thankful embrace. Vesper, meantime, had come to find out what was delaying us. The Weed, of course, had to begin babbling about what happened; at which, they both flung their arms around me, with Vesper calling me her dear tiger, and the two of them making such a fond fuss that I had to remind them where we were, neither the place nor time for a celebration.

Vesper finally hurried us to a vaulted stone tunnel, and we splashed through the drainage ditch. If Helvitius had ever imagined this to be the equivalent of Alph, the sacred river, he had badly misread Coleridge.

Compared with lakes of boiling tar and rivers teeming with aggressive reptilians, this was, bluntly, a sewer, which is the best that can be said for it—and the worst. Vesper and I had been in more perilous environments. Nevertheless, we were soaking wet, up to our knees in water so cold from the melting ice that my feet went numb and I shivered uncontrollably. What other substances were being poured into the stream, I preferred not to contemplate.

But the most irritating aspect of our progress through the ditch was: The Weed. Since I had saved him from a stifling death, he showed his gratitude by sticking to me like a long-legged, mop-headed barnacle.

"Mind your step, sir," he constantly advised me. "It's a bit slippery here. Are you sure you can manage it?"

On top of that, he insisted on putting a hand under my elbow, guiding me along as if I were a doddering grandsire. I was relieved when, at last, we reached open air and I could dodge away from him.

We emerged a little distance behind the sheds and rail spur. We skirted the catchment basin, no more than a large pool that I would hardly call a sunless sea. After so much darkness, the moonlight dazzled me as we sped from Xanadu.

Even then, I still feared that Helvitius had planned this, that he had foreseen our every move, and, like Olympian Zeus, was mocking our puny mortal efforts to escape.

Vesper halted to let us catch our breath. The Weed seized this opportunity to repeat in detail how I had saved his life; and I had to be thanked and congratulated all over again, with Mary and the twins joining in.

Only then did I realize someone was missing.

"Where is he?" I glanced around. "Where is Dionescu?"

"He told us to go on ahead," Vesper said. "He'll catch up with us. He's got something in mind—"

"Yes, leading Helvitius to us," I burst out. "Wretch! He has betrayed us again."

"Or he could be risking his life," Vesper said. "If he's not here soon—"

"We keep on our way," I said. "To Neopolis. As fast as we can."

"No," said Vesper. "We go back for him."

15

...

IF he's in trouble," Vesper said, "we can't just go off and leave him."

"Into the lion's jaws again?" I cried. "Dear girl, that goes beyond the bounds of common sense."

"I'm game for it," put in The Weed. "'Once more unto the breach, dear friends, once more,'" he proclaimed. "'Then imitate the action of the tiger; / Stiffen the sinews, summon up the blood—'"

"Enough Shakespeare," I interrupted. "The real Henry V never said such nonsense. No. Press on, away from here."

"Suppose he needs help?" Vesper insisted.

"Suppose he does not?" I countered. "Suppose it is yet another trap? Either way, let him look after himself. Be glad we are free of Helvitius—"

Until now, Mary had been silently listening. "Our dear Vesper is correct," she said to me. "We must face our responsibilities. Brinnie, the poor man may be risking his life."

"And so he should," I returned. "Did he not put our lives at risk? Let him risk his own for a change. I call that only fair."

"Brinnie, you occasionally astonish me," said Mary. "Is that the Philadelphia way? He is a fellow human being. More than that. He is a distinguished scholar."

To this, I had no conscionable reply. I finally, reluctantly, nodded agreement. "I forgot myself for a moment. Yes, it is the Philadelphia way."

"I knew Aunt Mary would help you see reason," said Vesper.

Our escape had brought us no great distance from Xanadu. As we clung to the shadows at the edge of rising ground, Vesper observed the dark shape of that bizarre structure, silent and brooding in front of us. I hoped to convince her to wait just a little while longer—Dionescu might find us from one moment to the next.

Vesper shook her head. "We can't lose any more time. Nothing's stirring. Helvitius doesn't know we're gone. If he did, he'd have his people swarming all over the place, searching for us. We have to be in and out before daybreak, too."

Then, I asked, what was her plan?

"I don't know yet," she admitted. "It depends on what we find when we're there. We'll start by going back the way we came."

Smiler and Slider took for granted they would accompany her; and, of course, so did The Weed. But he urged Mary and me to stay behind.

"Certainly not," said Mary as The Weed tried to persuade us to climb into the foothills and wait there. "What if we were to become separated? Furthermore, I have no desire to crawl through underbrush in the middle of the night."

I said the same. The Weed had that gleam in his eye. I had no intention of letting him loose without my supervision; no telling what that long-legged lunatic might decide to do.

"Stout fellow," said The Weed. "Good for you, sir. You'll be fine. I'll be with you all the way."

Vesper led us as we cautiously retraced our steps. We had scarcely reached the catchment basin—the "sunless sea"—when she suddenly halted.

In Xanadu, every chamber blazed with light, as if for some grand ball—which I knew was not the case.

"Turn back!" I cried. "Our escape is known!"

The outbuildings, too, were alight. Even as I watched, ribbons of flame uncoiled from one structure to the next. Slider observed the scene with professional interest.

"That," he declared, "would be gas."

"Gas, right enough," said Smiler. "I'd have to guess someone's tinkered with the pipes."

"Dionescu!" exclaimed Vesper. "He's trying to burn down Xanadu!"

"Away from here!" I seized Vesper's arm. The dear girl, I feared, still meant to plunge into the building and search for Dionescu. That same instant, the ground shuddered beneath my feet.

Next thing I knew, I was flat on my back. I expected my head to burst as one earthshaking explosion followed another. I could hardly breathe, as if the air were being sucked out of my lungs. Dazed, ears ringing, I sat up. The shock waves had tossed us all about like so many rag dolls. I could see nothing of Vesper, Mary, or the others through the heavy blanket of smoke.

I am sure the whole horrendous event took only moments; but time seemed to slow its pace as the massive walls of Xanadu crumbled and collapsed. Above the smoke, the stately dome rose aloft.

This crowning glory hung intact, as if suspended in the air, defying the law of gravity. But then—it must have been only seconds later—it shattered and fell in upon itself, crashing to the ground in a heap of rubble.

An eerie silence followed. I staggered to my feet. As best I could judge, we were all unharmed. Vesper, her face smudged, her clothing covered with dust and gravel, stood looking at the mountain of ruins.

"And that," she said, "was the Helvolene."

The Weed, of course, had to put in his oar. "'Huge fragments vaulted like rebounding hail,'" he murmured. "'Or chaffy grain beneath the thresher's flail . . . I would build that dome in air . . .'"

"Aye," said Slider. "Into the air it went."

"And that poor Dionescu," Mary said. "He did risk his life. I fear he lost it."

I bowed my head. Despite the cut and thrust of scholastic rivalry, one must always note the passing of a colleague. I resolved, once back in Philadelphia, to write his obituary and transmit it to the professional journals.

"Helvitius never wrote the ending to 'Kubla Khan,'" Vesper mused. "Instead, he turned a poem into a tomb."

It must have been dawn by now, but smoke and clouds of dust kept the whole area in darkness. Here and there, flames rose as pale orange smears. The stench of the diabolical Helvolene caught in our nostrils.

"Come away, dear girl," I said as Vesper proposed continuing to search for Dionescu. "There is nothing to be found."

The twins agreed that we should leave the grim sight immediately. For all we knew, there might be further explosions. Vesper, nevertheless, refused to give up the search; and The Weed eagerly took her side.

As I tried all my powers of persuasion, I could have sworn I heard the braying of a jackass. I stopped and stared. From some distance behind the wreckage of the sheds, leading a pair of donkeys, Professor-Doctor Dionescu trudged through the curtain of haze.

The poor fellow looked much the worse for wear. His mustache had been charred; burnt holes covered his garments. The donkeys appeared in better state.

With a glad cry, Vesper ran to greet him, as did we all. At sight of us, and in the embraces of Mary and Vesper, he beamed in the welcome he received. Seeing him relatively undamaged, Vesper plied him with questions. He was happy to offer explanations—for all his miserable condition, he was obviously pleased with himself.

"Helvitius, as I told you," he began, "conducted me on a tour of Xanadu's installations. He showed me the gas lines, the coke-fired furnaces, the storage sheds of Helvolene.

"When I left you at the drainage ditch, I made my way to the main control valve and increased the gas pressure, certain the pipes would burst, producing fires and explosions. In the storage sheds, I overturned canisters of Helvolene and spilled the contents in what I calculated would be the path of the flames. Since the behavior of that substance is unpredictable, I had time—though barely—to escape the devastation and to save our donkeys, as well.

"We must depart without delay," he warned. "There is a garrison of Ottoman troops in the vicinity. They could not have failed to hear the explosion. They may arrive at any moment. The colonel and his staff are in the pay of Helvitius. If found here, you will be questioned severely. Should your part in this become known, you will all surely face a firing squad— a welcome relief, considering what you will suffer before that."

In the light of this information, Vesper sensibly decided we should go to Neopolis. We were expected there, and The Weed would finally learn about his inscriptions.

I had, until then, stood a little apart. Now I approached Professor-Doctor Dionescu and did what my honor as a Philadelphian required.

"Your hand, sir," I said, extending my own. "I sincerely beg pardon for mistrusting you, and for whatever physical distress I may have caused you, and for my regrettable threat with the butter knife."

Dionescu courteously accepted my apology. I continued:

"Furthermore, I offer you my commendations. You have accomplished what none other has been able to achieve, not even Miss Vesper Holly. An individual of your intellect will appreciate the irony of Helvitius destroyed by the invention bearing his name."

"'For 'tis the sport to have the enginer hoist with his own petar,'" put in The Weed, three inches from my side. "That's Hamlet, sir."

"Please, Tobias, there is no need to state the obvious." I turned again to Dionescu:

"For myself, as a Philadelphian, I would have preferred to see that archvillain brought to stand before the bar of justice and face a stern reckoning in a proper court of law."

"So would I," Vesper added. "But, if that's the last of him, it's good enough."

16

...

OUR journey back to Neopolis took longer than I expected, for we moved carefully and cautiously, avoiding any Ottoman troops that might have been drawn to the area. Also—except for The Weed, who kept goading us on—we were exhausted by the past events and still caught up in reflecting on what we had witnessed. As my dear Mary had undergone such physical and emotional ordeals, I insisted on her riding one of the donkeys. Dionescu, still shaken, gratefully mounted the other animal.

I assumed he would leave us and return to the site at Vissarlik. Though he had not discovered the original Troy, his findings were, nonetheless, of archaeological interest.

"One day, perhaps, when it is safe to do so," he replied. "You should understand that Helvitius engaged all my workmen and paid their wages. Once they learn that I was responsible for his entombment and their consequent loss of income, I will not feel comfortable among them. They would have no compunction about cutting my throat.

"Miss Holly, I advise you and your party likewise to shun Vissarlik. The operative ordered to kidnap you—Captain Yaw-Yaw, as Professor Garrett refers to him—will doubtless return, expecting further compensation and instructions. The packet boat itself could well include untrustworthy hirelings among the crew."

"We'll have to take our chances on that," Vesper said. "I don't see any other choice."

"But there is," replied Dionescu. "Iskandria."

Vesper shook her head. "I've heard the name, but I don't know much about it."

"It is a small enclave," Dionescu said. "A French protectorate on this side of the Dardanelles Straits. It was established by treaty after the Crimean War as a kind of observation post, to keep a watchful eye on the doings of the Ottomans.

"It is not much farther than Vissarlik. You should be able to make your way overland without great difficulty. From Iskandria, you can obtain passage across the Aegean."

"A French colony?" said Mary. "I have certain reservations about their behavior, but the French do have some claim to a degree of civilization. They are agreeable enough, in their own peculiar fashion. I trust we would not remain there for an extended period of time."

"Iskandria it is, then," said Vesper. "But you, Professor-Doctor, what are your plans? Will you come with us?"

"Your offer, Miss Holly, is most generous," Dionescu replied, "but I hope to stay in Neopolis. I intend to observe their manners and customs, in a detailed study of the remnants of their ancient lore and language. Their culture has been handed down from before the days of Homer—preserved in amber, so to speak.

"It will provide me with a subject for a remarkable treatise in several volumes," Dionescu went on. "Nothing like it has been previously undertaken. I have every confidence its publication will come as an illumination to the academic world.

"Naturally," he added, "I shall credit the source of my research in copius footnotes."

"They'll appreciate that," said Vesper.

We arrived at Neopolis the following afternoon. Travel-stained and weary, we must have looked like the original ragged survivors of the Trojan War. As soon as the youngsters caught sight of Vesper and The Weed, they flocked around, whooping and capering, escorting us like an honor guard to the marketplace. Dressed in their best, they had been noticeably scrubbed and polished. What I had come to think of as their main street had been swept spotless. Garlands of flowers festooned the doorways and windows. Such an air of festivity filled the town that, had it been Philadelphia, I would have expected the police and firemen's brass band, along with our gallant First City Troop, to turn out in welcome.

We found all the local dignitaries gathered in their equivalent of our City Hall. I took it on myself to approach the council table and express our gratitude for the splendid reception they had laid on. I complimented them on the decorations, assured them we deeply appreciated their efforts, and felt honored by the display of friendship.

The *vassilos*, though clearly happy to see us, exchanged glances with his colleagues. I had barely touched on our dreadful experience at Xanadu when he raised a hand and began speaking. Vesper, nudging me to be quiet, stepped up and helped to interpret his remarks.

"He's glad we're here on this joyful occasion," she said, "but there's something he needs to explain."

The *vassilos* beamed and nodded as Vesper went on:

"First, he wants us to know that he, the village elders, and the keeper of the archives have all studied Toby's inscriptions. They agree: The writing goes back to the time of their earliest ancestors.

"As for Toby's translations," she said, "they're absolutely right."

The Weed made a lot of whooping and yipping noises. He threw his arms around Vesper and would have done likewise to the *vassilos* and everyone within reach if I had not hauled him back.

"It solves the puzzle!" he burst out. "Everything falls into place now. I can prove my theory. The alphabet went from east to west; the Greeks and the Cretans learned all they knew from the Trojans."

I did not wish to dampen his enthusiasm, but I tried to explain that historians rarely change their minds about anything. They would demand more than his translation of a few fragments of old inscriptions. They would, at the very least, require the decipherment of the complete alphabet. But he was too galvanized to pay attention to me. He only calmed down a little when the *vassilos* began speaking again.

"He says he's sorry if we misunderstood about the decorations," Vesper told me. "They aren't for us."

"They're not?" I said. "Then what are they celebrating?"

"A wedding," said Vesper. "Actually, a lot of weddings. This time of year, couples marry all on the same day. It's an ancient custom. The festival's tomorrow. They'll be honored if we attend."

"Marvelous!" put in The Weed. "Carrots, what I think— yes, well, what I think is: We ought to have a part in it."

"We do have a part," Vesper said. "We're the guests of honor."

"No," said The Weed, "I mean—really *be* part of it. You and I."

"Toby," said Vesper, "are you asking me to marry you?"

17

. . .

BY the time I pieced together what The Weed was trying to say, and Vesper's reply, Mary had already embraced the two of them. The *vassilos* and the Chamber of Commerce were all smiles. They had no comprehension of the actual words exchanged, but understood perfectly what had just happened. Proposals of marriage, I was sure, had not essentially changed since the days of their Trojan ancestors.

Mary surprised me—by her lack of surprise, as if she had expected this all along. I wondered if she had been told something she had not imparted to me. Or perhaps she had been aware of subtle clues that somehow escaped my notice.

"I think it's a beautiful idea," Mary said, "and so does Brinnie. Don't you, my dear?"

"Ah—the idea. As to that," I began, trying to collect my thoughts. Naturally, I assumed our dear Vesper would marry. But I envisioned that event as taking place in the distant future. Now I was grappling with the prospect of The Weed becoming, in a sense, an instant son-in-law.

"There are, ah, certain difficulties," I went on. "The legality of a marriage contracted in the outer reaches of the Ottoman Empire. An archaic ceremony, without proper certifications and licenses."

"Brinnie, that's the silliest thing I've ever heard," said Mary. "I'm sure it's every bit as legal as anything people do in Philadelphia."

Since my reasonable and sensible point had been dismissed out of hand, I cast around for additional expressions of wise advice and guidance.

"Be that as it may," I said. "In any case, these things should not be rushed into. Better to approach them leisurely, with ample time given to consideration of all aspects.

"In sum," I concluded, "one should contemplate the benefits of a prolonged engagement."

"Nonsense," Mary said. "They'll never get another chance like this. They have my blessing. And yours, Brinnie. Tell them so."

With everyone staring and waiting, I tried to formulate other questions. And found none. Vesper was looking at me, her old tiger, with such loving confidence that, at last, I nodded.

"My dear girl, I give you my blessing," I said. "And Tobias—you, too."

It has always puzzled me why occasions of great significance invariably, one way or another, end up in the hands of the ladies. As the father of the bride—or representing that position—I assumed my status would be recognized, that I would occupy some central place of honor and otherwise be given a role in the proceedings. This was not the case.

Once it was agreed that Vesper and The Weed would join the other wedding couples, and the twins, Dionescu, and everyone else had congratulated them several times over, a group of village women arrived. Next thing I knew, Mary and Vesper were whisked away, regardless of my questions and concerns.

"Never fret, Brinnie," Mary called to me. "We shall all be together in the morning."

I said I certainly hoped so. The Weed, too, was distressed to see Vesper so abruptly snatched from his side. Neither of us got much satisfaction from the *vassilos*, who only shrugged and assured us that from this moment the women were in charge, as had always been the custom. We were, in effect, left to our own devices.

He told us we would be welcome, as before, to spend the night in the *chiron*'s house; and so, at loose ends, we made our way there. The *chiron* and his wife were absent; only the goat was in residence. Smiler and Slider, never complaining, settled down to sleep. Dionescu stretched out in a corner. I would have gladly done the same, but The Weed kept nudging me to ask if I was comfortable.

"You've had a busy day," he told me, after prodding me awake for the third or fourth time to ask if I needed an extra blanket. "You should try to get some rest, sir."

Now that he had my full attention, he went on and on about his theory. When he temporarily exhausted that subject, he wandered forlornly around the room and finally went to sit in the doorway. The goat, meantime, snuffled at me until I gave up any hope of sleeping. I sat down beside The Weed, who was peering out at the darkened houses. From somewhere came sounds of female merriment.

"What do you think they're up to, sir?" he asked. "I wonder if we should go and find them. They might be glad for our company."

"Tobias," I said, "you will, in time, learn to let these matters alone."

"I suppose you're right." He nodded, then turned to me. "I didn't mean to surprise you, sir, about asking Carrots—but, you see, the idea just popped into my mind."

"With marriage proposals, that sometimes happens," I said.

The Weed kept quiet for a time, meditatively rubbing his head. Then he said:

"I truly do love her, sir."

"Of course you do. As you should," I said. "As do we all."

"I was afraid you wouldn't agree to it," he said. "It must have been a bit of a shock. It was good of you, giving your blessing."

"Tobias, my boy," I said, "'let me not to the marriage of true minds admit impediments.'"

The Weed's jaw nearly dropped to the floor. "Why—that's Shakespeare, sir."

"I know," I said.

The wedding, next day, had one thing in common with every wedding I had attended: It was late. Early that morning, some of the young men—in Philadelphia, they would have been, I assumed, the equivalent of groomsmen or ushers—came and took The Weed away with them. They instructed the rest of us to join the villagers at the market square. Though I was disappointed at having no part in the ceremony, we did receive a sign of distinction. We were allowed places in the first rank of onlookers. And there we waited, shifting from one foot to the other. When I feared my knees would become ossified, I became aware of some sort of activity.

A group of women filed out of City Hall and stood by a wicker trellis covered in greenery: the mothers of the brides, no doubt. I saw Mary with them, draped like the others in flowing white garments, a circlet of flowers at her brow. I caught her eye and she smiled happily at me.

I expected some preliminary speechifying from the *vassilos*, but he and his colleagues loitered in the background, doing not much of anything. I reminded myself this was women's business—the ladies' auxiliary, as it were; and, indeed, white-robed, wearing an elaborate headdress, the *chiron*'s wife stepped to the trellis. Along with her came a maiden carrying a basket of pomegranates. At the same time, wending their way up the street, a procession of the youngest village girls approached, singing as sweetly as any Philadelphia Sunday-school class.

Smiler and Slider watched entranced by the proceedings. Beside me, Dionescu hauled out a pad and pencil and busily scribbled notes.

"Most remarkable, most remarkable," he murmured. "I must investigate this in detail. My dear Professor Garrett, surely you appreciate the uniqueness of what we are witnessing."

Impatient to see Vesper and The Weed, I offhandedly replied that it was certainly not a Quaker ceremony or even Presbyterian.

"The priestess obviously represents Demeter, mother of

all growing things; the maiden, her daughter Persephone, kidnapped and taken to the Underworld. Observe the pomegranates . . ."

Dionescu rattled on about the tale every schoolchild knows. Before her mother could rescue her, Persephone had tasted a pomegranate and swallowed six seeds, condemning her to live with Hades six months each year while the earth lay barren, awaiting her return. A charming nature myth, but Dionescu grew all the more excited.

"Other elements are mixed in, stitched together from different sources." He scribbled away furiously. "It will take years of study to sort them out. Do you hear what the children are singing? I interpret it as: 'Like newborn lambs, come we athirst for milk.' There are other versions, and raging dispute over them. But, sir, I believe we are glimpsing parts of that most secret ancient ritual, the Orphic mysteries."

We probably were. In other circumstances, I would have paid better attention. At the moment, I was more interested in glimpsing Vesper and The Weed.

For now, following the children's choir, came the young wedding couples, side by side, perhaps half a dozen. The Weed was impossible to miss, head and shoulders taller than anyone around him. He had been fitted out with a tunic a little too short to cover his knobby knees, but otherwise quite presentable; the ladies, no doubt, would have called him handsome.

Vesper, of course, could never have been overlooked, whether in the wilds of Asia Minor or anywhere else. Her plain white robe, caught at the waist with a slender cord, seemed to float as light as air; her marmalade-colored hair, unbound, flowed loose around her shoulders. The dear girl could well have stepped gracefully in sandaled feet from a Grecian—in this case, Trojan—vase painting.

Smiler and Slider burst into applause. I would have done the same, but I realized such an enthusiastic outburst was as appropriate as cheering at a Quaker meeting.

I have, with Vesper's father, attended a number of rituals, the details in some cases best left unmentioned. In Illyria, Vesper and I were present at a remarkable pageant involving a mystical horse. But the wedding in Neopolis was the simplest and most beautiful of any I had seen. As I watched, the children's voices rose still more sweetly. Side by side, lovingly hand in hand, the couples approached the Mother of All Growing Things and knelt to receive crowns of flowers for the bride and laurel for the groom.

After that, I assumed it was over. The onlookers dispersed, the newlyweds joined in-laws and friends; Vesper and The Weed, faces shining, came to embrace us. But the *vassilos* hurried up to say there was more to come. Now, he explained, the whole village would celebrate. Naturally, we were invited.

From what I understood, it would not be too different from a Philadelphia wedding reception—refreshments laid on, pitifully humorous toasts, probably some dancing. Though never much of a dancing man myself, I supposed Mary might enjoy the occasion.

"You missed a big point," said Vesper, who had been closely following his words. "It lasts for a week. Nobody leaves the village; it would be a discourtesy. Then, when it's over, everybody needs three or four days to recover."

While Dionescu scribbled notes on his pad, Vesper and The Weed put their heads together in quick conversation. The prospect of a week's worth of festivities—I was already having misgivings.

"Brinnie," Vesper said at last, "I think we'd better head for Iskandria before the party begins."

"Would you be terribly upset, sir?" The Weed put in. "What it is, you see, Carrots and I would really like a proper honeymoon. If we first go back to Crete, I'll tell the museum fellows about the inscriptions. Then we're on our own. We can spend a month or so on the mainland, the Aegean islands, wherever we please."

"Brinnie and I can hardly go to Istanbul with the war on," Mary said, "but there is always Athens, Rome, Florence. Then, later, we all shall meet in Naples and sail home."

"I know you're disappointed, sir," said The Weed, "missing out on a grand party—"

"I am sure," Mary said, to my relief and gratitude, "Brinnie will gladly make that sacrifice."

Vesper, The Weed, and Mary went to return their wedding costumes and change into their travel clothing. The twins and I packed up the small amount of gear we had left at the *chiron*'s house. I already heard sounds of revelry as we made our way to City Hall again.

Professor-Doctor Dionescu, still with notepad and pencil, was there in a great state of excitement. He had been granted permission to stay in Neopolis as long as he pleased. The *chiron* and his wife, the *vassilos*, the Chamber of Commerce, the Municipal Council, and the village elders had gathered to bid us farewell and to offer parting gifts.

The *chiron* gave me a sack of his remedy against Shiva's Revenge. Smiler and Slider received small clay figurines of Demeter and Persephone; Vesper and Mary, amber necklaces. All common objects in the village, but curators of museums anywhere in the world would have cut each other's throats to get their hands on them.

As for The Weed, with much ceremony the *vassilos* handed him a stone disc a bit larger than the palm of my hand. Carved deeply into the surface were the outlines of a female figure wearing a bell-shaped skirt and high headdress.

"Astonishing," murmured Dionescu, craning his neck. "That is a representation of the Great Mother. It has always been considered purely a Cretan image. To find it here—unbelievable!"

"Lovely," said Vesper. "Anything on the other side?"

The Weed turned it over. He goggled at it, opened and shut his mouth like an insane fish. At first, I did not understand what the fuss was about. With The Weed still incapable of human speech, Vesper turned to me.

"Brinnie, do you realize what you're looking at? It's as good as the Rosetta stone. Here's the whole ancient alphabet with matching letters in Greek."

The Weed, meantime, was falling all over himself and blurting out his gratitude. I believe he would have spent the rest of the day thanking the *vassilos*, the Chamber of Commerce, and every inhabitant of Neopolis had I not taken his arm and suggested we should be on our way.

"This is a treasure," Vesper told the *vassilos*, as The Weed stowed his prize safely in his jacket. "You're really giving this to us?"

"In exchange for something else," he said. "When you are in your own country, tell that here a city was destroyed and our ancestors long gone into the earth. But also tell that we, their children, live on. And we are happy."

18

...

WE set off, then, for Iskandria. The Weed was practically walking on air. Every few steps, he would fish out his alphabet stone. Vesper, of course, had to admire and examine it along with him. I shared his enthusiasm, but only wished he would pay more attention to where he was going; our path was more difficult than Professor-Doctor Dionescu had led us to expect. This was not to detract from his eminence as a scholar, or the service he had performed in ridding the world of that diabolical inventor of Helvolene. In other respects, I found him alarmingly deficient.

We had, on his advice, left the donkeys in the village. They would, he assured us, be a hindrance in this particular terrain. To that extent, he was right. He forgot to mention long stretches of trackless overgrowth. He neglected to warn us of dry riverbeds with banks so steep we nearly went rolling head over heels. It never occurred to him to tell us there were no sources of drinkable water. Our throats grew so parched that The Weed gave up crowing about his prize. The twins doggedly pressed on. My dear Mary suffered in brave silence, but I could see she was beginning to falter. Even Vesper showed signs of strain; her face was drawn, a distressing flush covered her cheeks and brow. We all had lost the ability to perspire.

Dionescu had spoken of a rail line that we could follow to Iskandria. There was none. I welcomed nightfall, obliging us to halt and rest as best we could. I slept fitfully. Vesper, I suspected, did not sleep at all. When the rest of us awoke, I found her already on her feet.

"Brinnie, I've been thinking about it," she said. "We can't find the railroad . . ."

At first, I wondered if hardship had taken its toll and the dear girl, so rarely daunted, was about to surrender. Until she added:

"Because we've been looking in the wrong place. They wouldn't build it down here. They'd build it up there."

She pointed to a high, rocky escarpment rising sharply beyond the edge of the overgrowth. The twins had come to stand beside her, peering at the heights.

"A nice little climb," Slider observed as Smiler nodded.

My heart sank. "Dear girl, even if we manage to reach the top—suppose we find nothing?"

"I guess we'll just have to come down again," said Vesper. "So the sooner we start, the better."

We were ill equipped for mountaineering—that is to say, we were not equipped at all. What little gear we had included no ropes, crampons, or pitons. We could only inch our way painfully upward, grasping at whatever handhold or foothold the craggy face offered. The twins stayed in close support of Mary, who surprised me with an agility I did not know she possessed. The Weed, looking more than ever like a praying mantis, clung flat against the rocks. Vesper, usually as sure-footed as a mountain goat, nearly tumbled when a narrow ledge broke away.

I made the regrettable mistake of glancing down. I caught my breath; my head spun. If we found nothing, our descent would be close to impossible. It occurred to me we might be trapped halfway, unable to move in one direction or the other.

Vesper, arms and hands scraped raw, knickerbockers ripped by the jagged stones, had been gasping from her exertions. But now she gained her second wind and clambered steadily above us. The dear girl's determination drew us after her. Finally, we hauled ourselves onto a wide shelf cut into the flank of the mountain range.

In the middle of it, leveled to make a roadbed, a rail line wound along the contours of the hills. Sometimes it vanished beyond a sharp curve to reappear farther on.

"I thought we'd find it," Vesper said. "Too bad it isn't the Pennsylvania Railroad."

I estimated we still had a good long march ahead of us, probably twice as long as Dionescu had led us to believe. But we trudged wearily beside the tracks. We had not gone far, the morning sun had only begun to hammer us, when Vesper halted. She turned back, listening intently, shading her eyes toward the stretch of rails behind us.

A moment later, I, too, heard the rhythmic rumbling of powerful machinery. From around the bend, a locomotive hove into view, heading toward us at full speed, the passenger cars rattling and swaying after it.

Vesper calmly stepped onto the tracks. At sight of her, the engineer blew his whistle. From its high-pitched whooping and screaming, I judged it to be a train of French design. Vesper, I believe, could have ordered an avalanche to stop in midcourse; but a French locomotive—I was not too sure.

The Weed and all of us ran to pull her from the tracks, but she waved us away. The onrushing train bore down on her, the whistle frantically squealing. Vesper, hand uplifted, stood her ground.

I should never have doubted the dear girl's capability. In what seemed like a contest of wills, or a bullfight in Madrid, the locomotive skidded to a standstill, with a shower of sparks and a tormented grinding of the huge wheels. The engineer leaned out of his cab, shook a fist, and continued blowing his whistle. While jets of steam hissed from the cylinders, Vesper stepped up and rested one foot on the cowcatcher. She smiled and nodded her thanks at the furious engineer.

No sooner had the train halted than the entire staff of conductors, guards, ticket takers, porters, waiters in long white aprons came boiling from the carriages. In alarm and astonishment, some of the passengers poked their heads out the windows, while others climbed down from their compartments. Ladies in gloriously trimmed hats and feather boas, gentlemen in morning clothes and patent leather boots milled around the roadbed.

A dapper little man with a waxed mustache shouldered his way through the crowd. So much gold braid ornamented his uniform that he could have been one of Napoleon's field marshals. I assumed he was the conductor-in-chief.

"Sacré bleu! Nom d'un chien!" He burst out with a torrent of Gallic expletives, stamped his feet, and waggled such an aggressive finger at Vesper that The Weed hurried to her side and the twins adopted defensive postures.

"Good heavens, Brinnie," Mary whispered, "how have we fallen into the hands of the French?"

"Unthinkable! Unspeakable!" the conductor ranted on, while his outraged colleagues gathered around him. "Have you the comprehension of that which you have done?"

Vesper ignored this eruption. "It was very kind of your train to stop for us."

"Train?" the conductor flung back. "Do you call this a train? A common carrier? Ah, *non!* It is the jewel, the glory of transportational accomplishment! The Orient-Rapide!"

I could not withhold a murmur of admiration. I knew only sketchy details of this proud new conveyance. Under French management, with a consortium of European investors, the Orient-Rapide raced from Paris to Vienna, Bucharest, and finally Istanbul. Recently put in operation, it had already become legendary for its incredible speed and the elegance of its amenities. It was, in effect, a luxury liner on wheels.

Vesper replied sympathetically. The Orient-Rapide, she understood, represented one of the highest achievements of French civilization, ranking with the Louvre and the Paris Opéra. She charmingly offered our apologies for the inconvenience.

"But, monsieur, we have been voyaging under great diffi-culties," she added. "As a true child of France, *un enfant de la Patrie*, surely you will display the gallantry admired through-out the world."

The bosom of the Field Marshal—as I had begun to think of him—swelled against his buttons. "Gallantry, of course, is our national instinct."

"And so you won't deny us your assistance," Vesper went on, with maximum persuasiveness. "We need to reach Iskandria and, from there, make our way to our native city, Philadel-phia."

"What is it that you say?" The Field Marshal's eyebrows shot up. "You are from *la Philadelphie*? Home of the grand Benjamin Franklin! The Bell of the Liberty! I am honored—"

"Then you'll take us on to Iskandria?" Vesper said.

"Ah, regrettably, *non*. Impossible." The Field Marshal sadly shook his head. "The Orient-Rapide is occupied to complete-ness, no place unfilled, not a centimeter for one more passen-ger, let alone six. Mademoiselle, it breaks me the heart."

The Field Marshal, about to turn away, stopped and sud-denly brightened. "Do not yet despair yourselves. To us re-mains one last hope."

The sub-conductors and deputy sub-conductors had be-gun ushering passengers back to the carriages. The Field Marshal led us down the line of railway cars and indicated that we were to wait.

"I have every confidence he will come up with some-thing," remarked Mary as he hurried toward the rear of the train. "To give credit where it is due, the French have a ge-nius for the impromptu."

Ahead, the locomotive snorted, impatient to be en route. I feared the Orient-Rapide would depart without us; but, moments later, the Field Marshal was back. He motioned for us to step up into a vestibule at the end of the carriage. As reverently as approaching Napoleon's Tomb, he opened the door and allowed us to enter.

"But, monsieur," said Vesper, "didn't you tell us the train was full? Here's all the room in the world."

The car was, in fact, empty—empty, that is, of any occupant. Otherwise, it was quite filled with excellent furnishings, carpeting on the floor, and crystal vases of fresh flowers at the windows.

The Field Marshal spoke in a hushed voice. "The private carriage of His Excellency Count Max von Tarnhelm."

"Well, then," said Vesper, glancing around, "since His Excellency isn't here—"

"Ah, but he is," said the Field Marshal. "He is currently on the observation platform, enjoying his morning cigar—for His Excellency, a sacred moment. I dared give myself the audacity to intrude upon him. When I explained that you were *les Philadelphiens*, it enraptured him to invite you to spend, as his guests, the few hours remaining before we arrive at Iskandria.

"As a loyal citizen of *La Belle France*," the Field Marshal went on, "I am devoted to the glorious principles of liberty, equality, and fraternity. Did we not storm the Bastille and invent the guillotine?" He lowered his voice. "However, I recognize that only aristocrats of His Excellency's ancient lineage fully understand, in these crude modern times, the true nature of *noblesse oblige*.

"His Excellency will join you when he has finished fuming his cigar, and urges you to do him the honor of making yourselves comfortable. For my part, with the compliments of the Orient-Rapide, allow me to offer you a late breakfast. I suggest eggs Benedict, pâté de foie gras on toast points, and Beluga caviar with, naturally, a lemon wedge on the side."

"That should tide us over until lunch," said Vesper.

The Field Marshal hurried from the carriage. The train had started up and was gaining speed. We sank gratefully into the good, solid comfort of the overstuffed chairs and sofas. I could easily imagine His Excellency as, in a sense, resembling his furniture—a nobleman of the old school, with a walrus mustache and muttonchop side-whiskers.

I had half-closed my eyes, contemplating the promised breakfast—I believe we were all peckish for some nourishment—when the door at the far end of the carriage swung open. In stepped a figure wearing a white and gold military tunic, handsomely tailored with Austro-Hungarian flair, and the sash of nobility across his bemedaled breast.

I respectfully rose to my feet. Count von Tarnhelm had extended his hand in what I took to be a gesture of democratic fellowship. As he drew closer, I realized the outstretched hand gripped a Colt revolver aimed at Vesper's head.

"Please retain your seat, Professor Garrett. I suggest all of you do likewise," said Dr. Helvitius.

19

...

DID you expect Count Max von Tarnhelm?" Helvitius went on. "It is I—one of the many names I employ when traveling. All the world loves a lord, so I find the title most useful."

Vesper adapts quickly to the impossible. She motioned for The Weed to stay calm, and regarded Helvitius with icy disdain.

"You," she said, "have no business being alive."

"On the contrary," replied Helvitius. "I have a great deal of business demanding my personal attention. With the Russians, the Ottomans, and now, happily, with you. Thanks to benevolent fate, I was in my private suite, bombproof even against Helvolene.

"I emerged, as you observe, unscathed. My rail spur and rolling stock were still usable. I myself drove my steam engine to a junction with the Orient-Rapide. The same destiny that preserved my life brings us together once more. The hand of Atropos is at work in all of this.

"True, Xanadu is destroyed, but will rise again greater than before. You have given me the opportunity to rebuild it, as the poet says:

> *"Ah Love! Could you and I with Him conspire*
> *To grasp this sorry Scheme of Things entire,*
> *Would not we shatter it to bits—and then*
> *Re-mould it nearer to the Heart's Desire!"*

"Omar Khayyám," muttered The Weed.

"I look toward the future, not the past," Helvitius continued. "My oil holdings, my formula for Helvolene, and my numerous other residences remain intact. It is not in my nature to bear a grudge. I was disappointed more by your abrupt departure."

"My husband and I"—Vesper glanced at The Weed—"had a pressing engagement."

"Husband?" Helvitius appeared shaken, but took a firmer grip on the Colt and pointed it at The Weed. "A recent event, I assume. My felicitations to the happy couple. So soon a bride, so soon a widow? You may hold your life lightly, but not that of your nearest and dearest. Mr. Passavant is my assurance of your good conduct, and the good conduct of all of you. I do not wish to blow his brains out—it would soil the carpet and burden the maintenance crew—but, if I must, so I will."

My heart sank—not because of his threat, which I knew he would unhesitatingly carry out, but because I detected that familiar glint in The Weed's eyes. Who could guess what lunatic scheme he was turning over in his mind?

"Steady on, my boy," I murmured. "Calmness, by all means."

"Excellent advice," Helvitius said. "And so we shall comfortably pass the time until we arrive in Istanbul."

"What about the Russians?" said Vesper. "Suppose they break through and take the city?"

"I shall be there to welcome them with open arms," replied Helvitius. "Should the Ottomans win, I shall be the first to congratulate the Sultan on his victory. Either way, I am still the one to determine your fate—which, as I warned, may come upon you in any form. You cannot escape the moment of Atropos."

"That depends on what Atropos has in mind," said Vesper.

Helvitius shrugged. "I would regret parting company with you; but, if it is to my advantage, I may make a gift of you, a prize of war, to the Czar. A whimsical fellow, very inventive in his dealings with the ladies. Or—the Sultan would be delighted by two charming additions to his harem in Topkapi Palace.

"You and Mrs. Garrett would not be separated from your loved ones. That would be too cruel. They would be constantly in your presence as attendant slaves—with, you understand, certain necessary adjustments.

"There are many other choices," Helvitius continued. "My final decision presents an intriguing challenge, but one that I shall thoroughly enjoy."

The Weed was making aggressive noises under his breath. I had to wonder whether he or Helvitius posed the more immediate danger. Probably The Weed. I readied myself to grab him by the scruff of the neck.

That same instant, the Field Marshal stepped into the carriage. Two waiters bearing trays followed in his wake. The Field Marshal paused, surveying the scene. He seemed not the least perturbed, as if one passenger threatening others with a revolver was a common occurrence on the Orient-Rapide.

"Mademoiselle," he said, with admirable French poise, "shall I serve breakfast now?"

"To the devil with you and your breakfast," snapped Helvitius. "Go. Leave us."

"No!" Vesper snatched the opportunity to fling herself between Helvitius and The Weed. "Count Max von Tarnhelm? An impostor! He is Desmond Helvitius, murderer, arch-criminal—"

Vesper spoke with such sincerity and conviction that even an innocent would have confessed. Helvitius remained unruffled.

"Obey my command, monsieur." He tilted back his head and stared down his nose as if he had been an aristocrat to the manner born. "Be not misled by her appreciable charms. This young woman is an accomplished liar."

"Your Excellency, how can that be?" the Field Marshal protested. "A Philadelphian and also a liar? That is a logical contradiction."

"But she is no Philadelphian," Helvitius glibly replied. "None of them are," he went on—was there no limit to his brazenness? "They are inhabitants of that notorious den of evildoers, la Nouvelle Jersey. I know them of old. A ruthless gang of international thieves and hired assassins."

"Monsieur," put in Mary, "do we look like hired assassins?"

"Appearances can deceive." The Field Marshal hesitated. He frowned and glanced from us to Helvitius and back again. "The word of self-styled Philadelphians against the word of Count Max von Tarnhelm? An impossible decision.

"But, then, Your Excellency," he said, "a small question arises. How does it come to pass that it is you who are holding the revolver?"

"They attacked me," Helvitius retorted. "I am defending myself, you imbecile."

"Monsieur, I can resolve your dilemma," put in Vesper as the Field Marshal stood only more perplexed. "I ask you to imprison us."

"Eh? A curious request." The Field Marshal blinked. "But—this is the Orient-Rapide, not *la Bastille*. However, if that is what you wish, *oui,* the baggage car is available."

"Then lock us up," said Vesper. "When we stop in Iskandria, the authorities can sort it out. Oh—Count Max, as Helvitius dares to call himself, gets locked up, too. Your diligent investigators will find out who he really is."

The Field Marshal clapped his hands. "A compromise worthy of a Frenchman!"

"Outrageous!" blustered Helvitius. "I have affairs of the highest level, matters of state to settle. This is unacceptable."

"The truth must, on occasion, take precedence over politics," the Field Marshal declared. "If you are in fact Your Excellency, I will offer you my most groveling apologies. If you are not, I will offer you this"—he made a Gallic gesture—"for calling me an imbecile. In any case," he added, holding out a hand, "be so kind as to disarm yourself."

Helvitius, roaring curses at the Field Marshal, swung around to carry out his threat against The Weed. Vesper grappled with him, but he brutally flung her aside. I leaped to my feet, the twins did the same. My dear Mary moved faster than all of us. As Helvitius squeezed the trigger, she seized his wrist; the shot went wild, the bullet buzzed and ricocheted. The waiters dropped their trays and ducked, eggs Benedict spattered in all directions. Showing a vigor I did not know her to possess, my angel wrested the Colt from the villain's fingers and cast it away as if it had been some disgusting reptile.

Helvitius, weaponless, shouldered past the distraught waiters and burst into the adjoining carriage. The Field Marshal flapped his arms and shouted for him to halt.

The Weed went scrambling after Helvitius, but Vesper was already on the villain's heels. Leaving Mary and the twins behind, I joined the pursuit. Helvitius plunged through the wagons-lits—the sleeping cars—where passengers in various stages of dressing popped their heads from the curtained berths to gape at us.

The train, meantime, was gaining speed, no doubt to make up for its delayed schedule. With Helvitius now well ahead, we lurched after him from one swaying carriage to the next. Sub-conductors and assistant ticket punchers stumbled out of our way, carriage guards frantically blew their whistles. In the dining car, where passengers still lingered over breakfast, Helvitius seized passing waiters and sent them hurtling against us, seeking to hamper our pursuit. Indignant diners shouted protests as trayloads of food showered down upon them. Pressing on, Helvitius at last reached the locked door of the baggage car. He could go no farther.

"We have the beast at bay!" I cried, though I knew that Helvitius, trapped, would be at his most dangerous.

But he did not confront us. Instead, he bent and struggled with the connecting mechanism. To my shock, I realized he intended to uncouple the carriage and leave us stranded behind. Despite his efforts, however, he could not budge the heavy levers and linchpins. Abandoning his useless labor, he turned to a narrow iron ladder at the side of the car and, with an agility I never suspected, clambered to the roof.

I understood, then, that his goal was more ruthless than I had supposed.

20

...

HIS desperate scheme was clear to me now. He meant to do nothing less than attack the locomotive engineer; force him, and the fireman as well, from the controls; then commandeer the entire train and send it at full throttle through the Iskandria station, heedless of whatever death and destruction it might cause—and from there, at top speed, straight on to Istanbul.

Vesper, too, had understood his plan. She clambered up the ladder after him. The Weed, some paces behind, followed her example. Fearing for their safety, I did the same, though it took me some moments longer to gain the roof of the baggage car. The wind whistled in my ears; the Orient-Rapide plunged onward at such a rate that I could scarcely keep my balance.

Ahead, surprisingly nimble, Helvitius danced his way closer to the engineer's cab. The Weed, to my horror, lost his footing and sprawled full length on the roof, perilously close to being jolted off to the roadbed. By the time he scrambled up, Helvitius had already reached the coal tender.

Vesper leaped onto the gritty black pile. Helvitius was beyond her reach; she could no way come to grips with him before he gained the cab. But if he was out of reach, he was not out of range. The dear girl, ever resourceful, snatched up handfuls of coal and flung them at him with all her strength.

Helvitius, at first, chose to ignore these missiles. He shrugged them off and waved them away as if they were so many annoying insects. Vesper continued her barrage. As more and more of the jagged lumps found their mark, striking him sharply about his head and ears, he seized a shovel from the pile of coal.

Roaring furiously, he used this implement not only to deflect the shards that pelted him but, as well, to bat them back. He swung his shovel with such vigor that Vesper now came under attack from the very objects she was flinging at him.

The Weed was still too distant to help her. He stopped short. I saw him reach into his jacket and pull out a heavy object. I realized it was his treasured alphabet stone.

As Vesper bent to scrabble up more ammunition, The Weed assumed a loose-limbed stance. He drew back his arm, uncoiled it, and sent the disc flying past her head with a velocity close to that of a bullet.

I had long suspected The Weed of consorting with rowdy gangs of baseball enthusiasts and, perhaps, taking part in the game itself. Though unfamiliar with the finer points of what was rapidly becoming a national pastime, I had to look on with astonishment.

Helvitius, aware of a new and unfamiliar missile speeding directly at him, braced himself and brought up his shovel.

Yet, even as he swung, The Weed's disc, as if contrary to all the laws of physics, curved upward at the last moment. Helvitius flailed at empty air. The shovel dropped from his grasp as the alphabet stone solidly connected with his head. The impact sent him, dazed and staggering, off the coal tender onto the roadbed, to topple over the edge of the escarpment.

The Weed turned to me with that loopy grin of his: "I believe I struck him out, sir."

That moment, someone—my dear Mary, I later learned—had the presence of mind to pull the emergency cord. The Orient-Rapide screamed to a halt, throwing us all off balance; and I, in particular, flat on my back. By the time I got to my feet, Vesper had already jumped from the coal tender and was climbing down the face of the cliff, The Weed behind her.

I swung down to the roadbed. First to pop out of the train was the Field Marshal, brandishing his pocket watch and sputtering about interfering with railway timetables.

"Monsieur," I replied, "this was an emergency most dire. You will need all the details when you prepare your report for the authorities."

The Field Marshal shrugged. "Our passengers encompass jewel thieves, embezzlers, secret agents, fugitives from every imaginable law. Such events are, naturally, commonplace. If I were to write a report of each incident, I would have no time for my important duties."

"What?" I burst out. "This is no more than a trainload of felons?"

"Only the most elite, of grandest elegance," the Field Marshal assured me. "Monsieur, even felons require transportation. And who else can afford the Orient-Rapide?"

Mary and the twins had, by now, emerged. They hurried to join me.

"Oh, Brinnie, whatever have you been up to?" Mary cried. "Crawling on top of railway carriages? Dare I let you out of my sight for an instant?"

Smiler and Slider went to peer over the cliff. I had only begun to explain when Vesper hauled herself back to the roadbed.

"Too steep," she said, still catching her breath. "We can't climb all the way down. Even if we could, we'd never get back. But there's no sign of Helvitius. He must have dropped straight into the falls."

She pointed at the gorge far below, where a cascade plunged in a foaming curtain to the rock-studded river mouth.

"He got out of the Schuylkill River, he escaped being blown up by Helvolene. But this?" Vesper shook her head. "No, I don't expect we'll see him again."

I had, meantime, retrieved the alphabet disc lying undamaged by the railroad tracks. When The Weed reappeared, I handed it to him. "My boy, I believe this is yours."

As soon as Vesper understood that The Weed had risked his most prized possession, she went to fussing all over him, telling him it was the noblest thing he could have done and never to do such a thing again.

"Besides," she added, "a couple more lumps of coal and I'd have got him."

Not every day does one have the opportunity to rid the world of its most despicable villain. It was a moment for solemn reflection—or would have been, had we sufficient time. The Field Marshal, fuming about his schedule, hustled us into the late Count Max von Tarnhelm's carriage.

The Weed, naturally, had to make his contribution. "How does Milton phrase it?

> *"Sheer o'er the crystal battlements: from morn*
> *To noon he fell . . . and with the setting sun*
> *Dropped from the zenith, like a falling star . . . "*

"Well," said Vesper, "I suppose that's one way of looking at it. I'd say Atropos snipped his thread."

The Orient-Rapide, running late, stopped briefly at the Iskandria depot—that is, it barely slowed down enough to let us jump off. From what I could see, the harbor, with a couple of gunboats riding at anchor, was bigger than the whole town. It looked to be a pleasant little settlement, but we lost no time sightseeing. We easily found the governor's palace: a small compound of buildings in the Turkish style, the French tricolor waving from the flagpole in the courtyard.

Vesper, with her usual assurance, led us straight to the waiting room, where a few civil servants were doing not much of anything. Our ragged appearance, plus Vesper's request to see the governor, roused them to a state of consternation. However, once they learned we were from Philadelphia, an usher, uniformed more grandly than the Field Marshal, led us into a bright, airy office. The man at the desk glanced up, then jumped to his feet.

"Colonel Marelle!" Vesper ran toward him as he hurried from behind the desk to kiss her gallantly on both cheeks.

Colonel Marelle indeed he was, commanding officer of the Foreign Legion regiment we had met in Jedera years ago. His close-cropped hair had gone some shades grayer, his face pitted by a thousand sandstorms; but he was the same hard-bitten Legionnaire.

"Colonel no longer, Mademoiselle Holly," he said affectionately. "I have been—what is your term?—kicked up the stairs. For my sins, I am Governor-General Marelle."

"And I'm 'Mademoiselle' no longer," said Vesper, taking The Weed's hand. "Allow me to present my husband."

This set off an exchange of congratulations. Marelle was charmed to make Mary's acquaintance and heartily glad to see the rest of us again. I had always thought of him as the sort of fellow who would make a thoroughly decent governor; but, speaking of his new post, he did not seem especially joyful.

"Iskandria is a protectorate sufficiently inconsequential and out of the way so that I cause no difficulties for my masters in Paris. I am not exactly certain whom I am supposed to protect, or who is to protect the Iskandrians from their protectors."

I could easily imagine Marelle, honest and outspoken officer that he was, being a thorn in the side of the colonial administration and probably the whole Chamber of Deputies. But he did not dwell on his own concerns and dispatched the usher to bring refreshments.

"It would not surprise me to see you turn up in any corner of the world," he said to Vesper. "But, of all places, Iskandria?"

Vesper began her account of what had happened to us since leaving Hērákleion. As she described our encounter with Helvitius, Marelle's weathered face turned grave. He went to his desk and jotted down notes while Vesper told him about Helvolene and the scheme to gain oil fields throughout Asia Minor. He promised, at Vesper's urging, to write a full report.

"Helvitius is gone," Vesper added, "but he told us a lot of other people were in on the scheme. Helvolene—I understand the formula, it's simple enough. I could cook it up myself."

"Dear girl," I murmured, "please don't."

"My point," said Vesper, "is that sooner or later someone else is bound to work out the formula. Helvitius started something and we don't know where it ends. As we say in English, he's set the cat among the pigeons."

"I shall do my best to alert my government," Marelle replied. "However, I must tell you that no one ever reads my reports. To be fair about it," he wryly added, "I read none of their directives.

"As for your return to Crete," he went on, "passenger vessels are—how do you say it?—few and much distance between. But, as governor-general, I have certain small privileges. I am happy to place a gunboat at your disposal."

"Good heavens," said Mary, "the French navy? Are you sure it is completely safe?"

"It will only be a short voyage," said Marelle.

Vesper happily accepted the offer. The usher, meanwhile, had brought our refreshments, including bottles of champagne—I noticed it was Dom Pérignon, but here I had every confidence in it.

"To the new married and the old acquaintances." Marelle raised his glass. "And—*vive la Philadelphie* and her fairest daughter."

"*Vive la France,*" said Vesper.

21

...

FRANCE is a republic; but, aboard the gunboat, we were treated like royalty. Our passage across the Aegean was faster, more comfortable, and better nourished than our crossing with Captain Yaw-Yaw. Also, the officers and crew presented the newlyweds with French sailors' hats. I found the red pom-poms a touch frivolous—but with a certain flair. Vesper and The Weed looked very dashing in them.

We anchored at Hērákleion only long enough to collect our stored baggage and to take loving leave of the honeymooners. Mary confessed a lack of interest in prolonging our own tour:

"Really, my dear Brinnie, after all we've been through, ancient ruins and statues without heads or limbs have lost a great deal of their charm."

A little wilted around the edges myself, I quickly agreed. The gunboat captain obligingly took us all the way to Naples. There, as if to make up for previous inconveniences, by blessed coincidence the *City of Brotherly Love* was preparing to sail for Philadelphia. We booked passage immediately.

It felt odd, after all our other journeys, that Vesper was absent at this happy homecoming. Once again in Strafford, I could not concentrate on my Etruscan history. Instead, as a civic duty, I drafted a long communication to our new chief executive, Mr. Rutherford B. Hayes. I pointed out, as Vesper had done with Governor Marelle, the perils facing the world. I dispatched the twins to Washington City to deliver this document personally.

President Hayes declined to receive them. They were obliged to hand over my report to an office flunky.

"Too bad General Grant isn't there," grumbled Smiler. "He and Miss Vesper rubbed along pretty well."

"Especially after she saved his life," said Slider. "Aye, he'd have seen us straightaway."

After a few weeks, an answer did arrive: a pre-printed form letter from the president thanking me for my support and urging me to vote for him in the next election.

"Not like the good old days," muttered Slider.

"It never is," said Smiler.

Throughout the autumn, we did get letters. Much delayed in the mail, the news was already ancient history. Vesper and The Weed had made an excursion to Hissarlik and met Herr Schliemann. His findings at the real site of Troy were quite remarkable, but none compared in significance to The Weed's alphabet disc. They had also gone to Illyria—still at peace, thanks to Vesper. They planned to visit Drackenberg and admire the world-famous *La Fortunata,* one of Leonardo da Vinci's greatest portraits, which Vesper had rescued from a cheese box. After that, they might press on to North Africa and Jedera.

Vesper, I understood, wished to share her girlhood memories with The Weed. But her messages reminded us all the more of her absence. The house itself seemed twice as big and full of echoes. As I remarked to Mary, I even missed The Weed.

"I miss the dear boy, too," Mary said. "He reminds me so much of you. In your younger days, naturally."

"Perish the thought!" I exclaimed. "I see no resemblance whatever. For one thing, I never bounced."

"You've forgotten, dear Brinnie." Mary smiled lovingly. "But I remember you very well."

Some weeks passed without further word. I started again on my Etruscan history, as much to pass the time as anything else. That afternoon, shrieks from downstairs jolted me out of my contemplation. I sprang up, fearing some domestic disaster.

In came Vesper and The Weed, looking marvelously fit, with Mary, Mrs. Hudson, and the twins crowding behind. Astonished, I stammered—or babbled—that I was overjoyed to see them both.

"Both?" Vesper said. "I guess you didn't get our last letter. Dear Brinnie, there's going to be three of us."

Our winter holidays were happier than they had ever been. As for the outside world, late in January our illustrious

Philadelphia Courier-Standard reported that the Russians had won the war with the Ottomans (the writer insisted on calling them "Osmans") and devoted nearly a paragraph to it. I was more interested in Vesper's coming event.

I mark our official exile as beginning in early summer, when Mary suggested: "Brinnie, my dear, why don't you and Toby go and help the twins with—whatever it is they're doing."

Mary spoke with utmost affection. Still, it sounded to me as if she were advising us to play outdoors and fly kites while the ladies attended to significant business. I suspected we would not be welcome amid household activities. From then on, The Weed and I were thrown back on our own resources. To my surprise, The Weed asked me to instruct him in the art of beekeeping. Which I did. In exchange, he offered to show me his decipherment of the stone disc from Neopolis.

As a result, The Weed and I spent much of our time in my study. He was, I must say, excellent at his work. I came to enjoy my days with him. I even got used to his bounciness. Perhaps Mary's observations about us were correct.

Only once was he anything less than cheerful. On the night it became clear that the great occasion could happen at any time, Smiler and Slider stood sentry duty at Vesper's door in case they were needed for unforeseen errands. Vesper wanted nothing to do with doctors. The admirable Mrs. Hudson was a skilled midwife, Mary an unflappable assistant. The Weed and I had been closely confined to my study. He did not bounce. Instead, he sat with his elbows on his knees, looking less like a praying mantis and more like a frightened ten-year-old.

"It's going to be all right, isn't it, sir?" he asked for the sixth or seventh time—I had lost count. Setting aside any apprehensions of my own, I assured him it would be.

"As the Swan of Avon puts it," I said:

> *"Jack shall have Jill;*
> *Nought shall go ill . . . "*

He brightened. "*A Midsummer Night's Dream.* Yes, '. . . and all shall be well.' Thank you for that, sir."

"My boy," I said, "my very dear boy, you are welcome."

I must have dozed in my chair then, for, next thing I knew, Mary was nudging me. She hurried me to Vesper's room. The Weed was already there, with the twins and Mrs. Hudson, all with besotted grins; and Vesper, in a nest of pillows, grinning wider than anyone.

"Here's Mary Brinton," she said. "She wants to meet you."

I have never been able to tell the difference between one infant and another. Not so, in this case. Mary Brinton had a generous head of unmistakably marmalade-colored hair. Also, I assumed that newborns had no ability to focus their attention. Yet, as I bent to peer at her, she fixed me squarely with a pair of green eyes. Then she reached up and seized my nose with such a grip that I could hardly disengage myself; nor did I want to.

"You're my dear old tiger," said Vesper, her own green eyes shining. "You'll be hers, too."

"Goodness me," put in Mary, "it will be years before the darling child even thinks about dashing all over the place."

"Of course, of course," I said.

I can wait.